PUDDING
BAG *School*

THE BIRTHDAY WISH

KT-557-123

PUDDING BAGSCHOOL

THE BIRTHDAY WISH

Hilary McKay

Illustrated by
David Melling

a division of Hodder Headline plc

A Catalogue record for this book is available from
the British Library

ISBN 0 340 69833 0

Typeset by Avon Dataset Ltd, Bidford-on-Avon, Warks

Printed and bound in Great Britain by
Clays St Ives plc

Hodder Children's Books
A division of Hodder Headline PLC
338 Euston Road
London NW1 3BH

CHAPTER ONE

Simon Percy was ten years old on the last day of the summer holidays. That year, instead of a birthday party, he had a picnic in the park.

"Then you can ask a crowd," said Gran.

Simon was not at all sure that he wanted a crowd. He thought there could not be a more unlucky day of the year to have a birthday. He knew exactly what the people invited would be sure to talk about, and he did not think he could bear it.

That was why the birthday picnic ended up having only two guests, Dougal McDougal and Madeline Brown. Simon was almost certain he could trust Dougal and Madeline not to ruin his birthday, but just to make sure he added an extra line to the top of their invitations.

PLEASE ONLY COME IF YOU PROMISE NOT TO TALK ABOUT TOMORROW

All afternoon Madeline and Dougal had managed to avoid the subject. It was Simon himself who said the word.

"School," said Simon. "School in the morning."

The picnic was spread out under an enormous beech tree and by this stage everyone except Gran had stretched out flat on the grass to take the weight off their stomachs.

"School in the morning," said Simon again.

Madeline and Dougal nobly remained silent. Simon raised himself on his elbows and glanced quickly across at them. They gave no sign of having heard, but Gran reached out a comforting hand. "Surely not!" she murmured, rubbing her great-grandson's hair as she spoke, and noticing vaguely how much it looked and felt like the trodden, end-of-summer turf of the park. "Surely not! You worry too much Simon! Come now, it is time for the cake!"

Madeline, Dougal and Simon sat up at once, recognising that birthday cakes are special things, not quite of the ordinary world. The solemn lighting of the candles was watched in silence. In the bright September sunshine the flames were almost invisible but even so there was a breathless pause when the last one trembled uncertainly, and a sigh of relief as it recovered again.

"Now then!" said Gran, and led the singing of Happy Birthday.

"Thank you," said Simon, when the song and the three shrill cheers that followed had ended.

"You *could* have asked more people if you'd wanted Simon," said Gran, as if to apologise for the unsubstantial nature of the singing.

"I think just a few is much friendlier," said Madeline, but Dougal, with typical tactlessness, remarked, "Most people have more family than Simon! That's the difference!"

"Shut up Dougal McDougal!" said Madeline at once.

"He doesn't mind," said Dougal. "Do you Simon?"

"No," said Simon, who actually minded very much indeed, but had learnt to accept the fact that people would always be endlessly fascinated by the story of his missing parents.

"Well then," said Dougal robustly. "We can't not talk about *everything*! And Simon's mum and dad! *Very* weird! Disappeared, just like that!"

"No Dougal, they did *not* disappear!" corrected Gran. "They went on holiday when Simon was six weeks old."

"Yes, but what a holiday!" exclaimed Dougal.

"A ten day hot air ballooning holiday," said Gran. "Or supposed to be!" and she sighed regretfully.

"Are you *sure* it was days?" asked Madeline, after the moment of silence that followed.

"Perfectly sure my dear."

"Because if it was years," persisted Madeline, "Not days, they'd be back quite soon, wouldn't they?"

4

"I never thought of that!" exclaimed Simon excitedly, but Gran shook her head.

"I should never have agreed to years," she told Madeline kindly but firmly. " 'Ten days,' they said. 'The foothills of the Himalayas! It is the chance of a lifetime!' 'Well,' I told them (foolishly, although you were a charming baby Simon), 'In that case you had better go and do not hurry back if you are enjoying yourselves . . .' and then nothing but that postcard when Simon was three . . . 'Wish You Were Here!' . . . Oh dear!"

"Hadn't Simon better blow his candles out?" asked Dougal practically, seeing that the rest of the party were lost in thought. "They've nearly burnt down to the icing!"

Gran glanced at the cake and said that Dougal was quite right.

"The sooner the better Simon!" she urged, but Simon hesitated, saving up the moments that were left. When the candles were gone it would be the end of his birthday tea, the end of summer, and he would be officially ten years old.

"Ten years gone in a flash!" said Gran.

It did not seem a flash to Simon. It had taken all his life. He sighed, and the sigh mixed up with a puff of wind and the flames blew out. There was a brief scattering of sparks across the chocolate icing and Simon almost missed his birthday wish. Just in time he caught it back, and knew at once exactly what it ought to be. He squeezed his eyes tight shut to help him recall the exact words of Madeline's astonishing suggestion, and opened them with such a solemn expression on his face that Dougal could not resist asking, "What did you wish, then?"

"Never tell," said Gran. "Never tell wishes until they come true! Did I hear you mention something was happening in the morning, Simon?"

"School," said Simon.

"School, school, I must not forget!" said Gran, forgetting at once.

The first crisp leaf of autumn came tumbling down. It landed on the birthday cake, fiery gold and shaped like a star. Miraculously, and for the first time that summer, Simon forgot about school as well.

Gradually the afternoon turned to evening and the park began to empty.

Dougal McDougal's seven grown-up sisters arrived in a posse and took him captive. Madeline Brown's professor father wandered over to the beech tree, peered at Simon and Gran and Madeline, asked plaintively, "Is this *supposed* to be happening?" and looked very relieved when they assured him that it was.

"Do help yourself to cake," said Gran.

"That is most kind," answered Madeline's father, "but I am afraid I find refined carbohydrates give me such pronounced irregularities of nerological stability..."

("Sweet things go to his head," translated Madeline.)

"... that I follow a strict diet of complex carbohydrates, amino acids and albumen..."

"Boiled eggs and carrots," explained Madeline and gave a little sigh. Boiled eggs and carrots were consumed in vast quantities in Madeline's house. Simon's birthday tea had been a very nice change.

"Thank you Mrs Percy, and thank you

Simon," she said. "I've had a lovely time."

"My wife," said Madeline's father to Simon, ". . . er *Mrs* Brown . . . Madeline's *mother* . . . has asked me to wish you a very happy, er, a very happy. . ."

"Birthday," supplied Madeline. "Where *is* mother?"

"Parachute jumping," said her father as he solemnly shook Simon's hand. "Suffers from pathological adrenalin craving . . ."

Madeline gently but firmly began to lead him away.

". . . interesting affliction . . ."

"Mother just likes the excitement," Simon heard Madeline say soothingly, and then she turned to wave goodbye and was gone.

It seemed suddenly lonely under the beech tree without Dougal and Madeline. Simon was glad to help pack up the remains of the picnic and prepare to go home. There, while Gran sipped China tea from her special pink cup, he arranged and admired his birthday presents.

He had five. A large box of Black Magic

chocolates from Dougal. Invisible ink felt pens given by Madeline. From Gran a pair of binoculars, a small cockatoo, and a book called *A Practical Guide to Space Exploration*. Simon opened the chocolates, wrote an invisible ink thank you letter to Gran, polished the binoculars, coaxed the cockatoo out of her cage and tidied *A Practical Guide to Space Exploration* carefully out of sight.

"What lovely books you have!" Madeline had exclaimed earlier that afternoon, but Simon did not think they were lovely. Gran chose books not for pleasure, but in the hope of equipping her great-grandson with an independent and enquiring mind. She was ninety-five and his only known relation, and she strongly suspected an independent and enquiring mind might be very useful to Simon one day.

Madeline had read aloud the titles of Simon's books:

"A Child's Guide to Modern Technology
Metal Work for Beginners
Junk Modelling that Works
Navigation for Nine Year Olds

Understanding Everything
Self Help for the Under Sixes
Anybody Can Do Anything and *How Does It Go?"*

There was also *Where the Wild Things Are* which Gran had bought by mistake, thinking it was Natural History and might perhaps remind Simon of his parents. It was the only one that he had read.

That night Simon dreamed of space exploration. Also of candles and cake. Also, and horribly, of Mr Bang Bang Jones, sole reason for the extra line on the birthday invitations. Mr B. B. Jones (often known as Old Bang Bang) was the Headmaster of Pudding Bag School, and he was also, and most unusually, what Dougal McDougal had once described as a second-hand spaceman. He used to be an astronaut.

The children of Pudding Bag School had long since discovered that second-hand astronauts made very worrying headmasters, and Mr Bang Bang Jones had made up his mind from the start that Headmastering in no way compared to exploring unknown galaxies. Still, he had hopes of it one day leading to higher things. His books on Headmastering Techniques sold very well, and the children (who he treated as alien life forms) were quite useful for research purposes if kept properly under control . . .

Simon turned restlessly in bed. Last term his teacher had left suddenly and with no explanation (this was not at all unusual in Pudding Bag School) and Mr Bang Bang Jones had taken over the class instead . . .

"School tomorrow," moaned Simon in his dreams.

Across the street the church clock chimed three, and Simon, who had been tossing and turning on the edge of sleep, woke up. Three o'clock, and school tomorrow! No! Even worse, school today! School in six hours' time and he had nothing prepared! Simon rolled sleepily out of bed and groped through cupboards and drawers until he had unearthed his school uniform.

The cockatoo stirred and rustled like a leaf in the wind.

Simon piled the clothes on a chair, climbed into bed, looked at them, climbed out, put them on, and finally lay back down again, his arms and legs arranged in straight lines, like a stick man falling through space, so as not to crease anything. The church clock struck four.

Outside the window a shooting star dropped through the sky. Simon curled into a sudden tight ball and fell fast asleep.

CHAPTER TWO

Simon's Gran was not very good with time. She had lived through so much of it. Tens of thousands of days, hundreds of thousands of hours. A few minutes here or there meant nothing to Gran anymore; after all she had lived through millions. That was why she simply could not understand the fuss Simon was making about a little bowl of cereal.

"You must eat breakfast," she told him patiently.

"But I shall be late!"

"Breakfast is important!"

"Old Bang Bang Jones thinks being on time is important," said Simon as he chewed and chewed on shredded wheat that refused to allow itself to be swallowed. "Old Bang Bang's terrible, Gran!"

"When things were terrible," said Gran slowly, looking far, far past Simon into the tens of thousands of days behind her. "When they were terrible I used to say, 'This will pass.' And it did. It always did. It always does."

Simon abandoned his shredded wheat and got up to give Gran a sudden tight hug. It felt to him as if he had been ten for a very long time.

Once he was out of the house it seemed that Gran might have been right after all. Any desire to rush to school suddenly deserted Simon and he plodded along Pudding Bag Lane in an increasing muddle of fear. He could tell by the empty pavements how late he was but instead of hurrying he went more and more slowly. There was a small sweet shop outside the school gates and he paused and inspected its dilapidated window display with the same feverish interest that people visiting the dentist have for the waiting room magazines.

Nothing looked very enticing. There were ancient boxes of tuppenny chews, bubble-gum in faded wrappers, damp flying saucers and melting red bootlaces. The back of the shop, as always, disappeared into darkness. A notice on the door read "OPEN when absolutely necessary". It was, as usual, locked.

Simon turned his attention to a poster in the window. It was an advertisement for an agency. Until now he had never given it more than a glance but now he read it all through.

SIMPLY THE BEST!
For Household Pets, Professional Staff,
Vacuum Cleaner Parts.
Dry Cleaning, Spring Cleaning, Caretakers
and Cooks.
Fine Jewels, Fireworks, First Class Free
Advice.

Enquire Within! All Needs Supplied!
Everything Guaranteed Best In All The
World!

Underneath, in ordinary hand writing, someone had added, (Cockatoos and Caretakers temporarily out of stock).

Simon read it three times and such was his state of mind that he did not even notice the reference to cockatoos.

Assembly had finished by the time Simon finally arrived at school. Register was over and the whole class were seated. If it had not been for Dougal McDougal he would have been lost, but Dougal had saved him a seat and loaned him a pencil and whispered the new teacher's name.

"Miss Leatherbottom!" whispered Dougal McDougal.

From the diary of Simon Percy. Tuesday 9th September

We have got a new class teacher. NOT MR BANG BANG JONES!

Simon outlined the words in red and drew stars and rockets round the edge. He could hardly believe his luck. No Mr Jones with his thunderous noise and his smoking, volcanic silences. No Mr Jones, staring and glaring and handing out punishments. No Mr Jones with his cries of, "Silence! Hard work and Silence! Simon Percy! Wake up! You might be the original Pudding Bag!"

Last term Mr Jones had compared Simon's brain to the original pudding bag of Pudding Bag Lane so many times that its owner had begun to have serious worries.

They have put me in Class 4b, wrote Simon, still worrying. *Why have they put me in Class 4b? Is Class 4a the brainy ones class?*

"Yes, dear?" said the new teacher, seeing a hand waving about at the back of the room.

"*Is* Class 4a the brainy ones class?" asked Simon.

"I hope not," said the new teacher, smiling very kindly at Simon.

Our new teacher has given us each a book to be our diaries to fill in whenever we have an empty moment. Dougal McDougal who is my best friend has filled in his for the week already. He says he knows what will happen. Our new teacher is . . .

Simon Percy paused for several moments, staring into space.

. . . *magic* wrote Simon, finding the right word at last.

"I've been scared all holiday that we would have Mr Jones for Class teacher again," he whispered to Dougal. "It spoilt the summer."

"Old Bang Bang," said Dougal McDougal scornfully. "He's nothing but a second-hand spaceman! I don't know why everyone's so frightened of Old Bang Bang! I bet *she's* not!"

Dougal nodded towards the stock cupboard where the new teacher, invisible except for a pair of sparkling green shoes, was busy with an enormous list.

"I bet . . ." began Dougal, and stopped as abruptly as if he had been switched off.

A sudden noise had shaken the windows. The whole class froze and the new teacher's startled face popped hurriedly round the stock cupboard door.

"Whatever . . .?" she began.

"It was Mr Jones' office door," Dougal McDougal told her, recovering his assurance. "Slamming!"

"It sounded like the roof falling off!"

"And that's him coming down the corridor. That smacking noise. It's his feet."

"I . . ."

"Everyone's scared of him," continued Dougal, "except me and Madeline Brown . . ."

"Madeline Brown?"

"The one with plaits. He's coming this way."

"Madeline Brown, please open the door," said the new teacher, suddenly taking control. "Then the headmaster need not knock . . ."

"He never knocks," said Dougal, helpful to the last. "He just gives a wopping great bash . . ."

The wopping great bash came just at that moment and would have flattened Madeline Brown completely had not her teacher swooped across the room and rescued her just in time. Mr Jones had arrived.

"I do not encourage," Mr Jones told Madeline pompously, "skulking behind doors. Ah! The new teacher!" he said, glaring at Miss Gilhoolie. "Grave doubts! Grave doubts!"

"I beg your pardon?"

"Still, it is a temporary position, depending upon satisfaction . . ."

"I am sure I shall be satisfied," said the new teacher not very calmly. "Madeline dear, go and sit down since you are not hurt."

"Mutual satisfaction!" interrupted Mr Bang Bang Jones who was clearly on the point of explosion. "I will warn you in advance that Class 4b, Pudding Bag School, Pudding Bag Lane, is by far the worst in the school as regards application, concentration, multiplication, subtraction, coherent explanation and remembering to bring back notes from home. Not to mention containing the original Pudding Bag! In fact it was because of their exceptionally primitive behaviour that I made use of them for my research last term."

"I am very much looking forward to working with them!"

"Alien life forms in all but habitation," continued Mr Bang Bang Jones, pinky purple with crossness at being interrupted, "I shall need them again so do not spoil them, Miss er . . . Miss er . . . Young Miss! Stick to my regime if you please! Hard work and silence! Also Science, Mathematics, form filling, and periods of extreme boredom to prepare them for future life. But science is the thing! I should like to see them all exploring Outer Space!"

"They are far too young," said the new teacher unhelpfully, and clearly not at all pleased at being addressed as Young Miss. "Now Mr Jones, I have been going through the stock cupboard and making a list of our most urgent requirements. I find we need poster paints, coloured paper, scissors, glue, glitter, new brushes, gold and silver ink (for marking), a new sweet tin, a new biscuit tin, story books (at least two hundred), a new computer, a piano, Christmas decorations, and comics and games for wet playtimes."

"What? *What!*" shouted Mr Bang Bang Jones.

"Poster paints, coloured paper, scissors, glue, glitter, new brushes, gold and silver ink (for marking), a new sweet tin, a new biscuit tin, story books (at least two hundred), a new computer, a piano, Christmas decorations, comics and games for wet playtimes, and games equipment."

"*Games equipment*?"

"Footballs, netballs, tennis balls, rounders bats, hoops, mats, ropes and a trampolene. Skittles, sacks, eggs and spoons . . ."

Mr Jones, who had been staring at her with a mixture of fury and astonishment on his face, suddenly smiled.

"Most amusing," he said, and his eyes looked to Simon like two empty screens. "Most amusing," and without another word he stalked out of the room.

Class 4b sighed with relief.

"What a lot of huffing and puffing!" said the new teacher cheerfully.

"I told you she wouldn't be scared of him," whispered Dougal McDougal.

Miss Leatherbottom is very pretty. Her hair is the

colour of the leaf that fell on my birthday cake
and her dress is shining green.

Your diaries are private matters, she said to us
all. So I shall resist reading them. But Simon why
do you keep asking me how to spell leather bottom?

Because I am writing about you, I said.

Oh, she said, but I have not got . . . why do
you think? . . . WHAT are you putting Simon
Percy?

And then she read this diary although she had
just said they should be private. And then
she said Copy This Down and wrote on the
blackboard.

My class teacher's name is Miss Gilhoolie NOT
MISS LEATHERBOTTOM.

Gran's little house was one of those which
backed onto the playing fields of Pudding
Bag School. At morning break Simon ran out
into the playground, looked up at his bedroom window and there was the cockatoo,
looking back down at him.

"Oh Miss LeatherGilhoolie!" cried Simon,
rushing back into the classroom in great
excitement. "Come and see my cockatoo!"

Too late he saw that she was not alone.

"Your teacher does not wish to see your cockatoo!" snapped the furious voice of Mr Bang Bang Jones.

"Of course I wish to see Simon's cockatoo," exclaimed Miss Gilhoolie immediately.

"Your teacher is about to make a very important purchase on behalf of you all," continued Mr Jones, ignoring her completely. "A signed edition (in three volumes) at a mere forty-nine pounds ninety-five pence per volume of my own privately published work," and he waved his hand to indicate three enormous black books arranged on Miss Gilhoolie's desk.

PRACTICAL PUNISHMENTS

ALL FULLY TRIED AND TESTED

WITH COLOUR ILLUSTRATIONS

BY

B.B. JONES (SIR)

"But I believe in Rewards and Encouragement," protested Miss Gilhoolie.

"These books will change your mind for ever," replied Mr Bang Bang Jones. "And the colour illustrations are Works of Art in themselves."

"They sound absolutely dreadful!"

"Thank you, thank you!" said Mr Bang Bang Jones, looking pleased for the first time and rubbing his hands together in delight. "They *are* absolutely dreadful. That is the whole point. And how many sets would you like to purchase? One for home and one to keep in the classroom of course. And some for Christmas presents? Or as Warnings to Close Friends? All profits to a private very good cause."

"What very good cause?" asked Miss Gilhoolie suspiciously.

"A *private* very good cause," repeated Mr Jones peevishly, not wishing to explain his secret hope of saving enough money to bribe NASA into letting him back into their rockets. "Shall we say three copies, Miss Gilhoolie? Nine volumes?"

"I think *not*, Mr Jones," said Miss Gilhoolie, very politely. "And now please excuse me. I have been invited to see a cockatoo."

Mr Bang Bang Jones looked shocked. "Kindly explain yourself!" he said.

"I shall not be buying any of your books," explained Miss Gilhoolie, very kindly indeed.

"But no one has ever refused before!"

"It is a great shame that I should be the first."

"Impertinent and unprofessional!"

"Mr Jones!" said Miss Gilhoolie reprovingly. "Come Simon!"

"You will regret this Young Miss!" roared the headmaster at her departing back, but Miss Gilhoolie simply shrugged a sparkling shoulder and waved a cheerful hand.

"Miss Leatherbo . . ." began Simon when they were half way across the playground. "I mean Miss Gilhooliebottom . . . I mean Miss LeatherGilhoolie?"

"Yes Simon?"

"Couldn't you buy those books? The other teachers do."

"No Simon."

"It would please Mr Jones. Then he might not be so cross."

"I expect there are other ways of pleasing Mr Jones," said Miss Gilhoolie. "What does he like, besides selling books?"

"Nothing I don't think. Well, space, I suppose."

"He has quite a large study..."

"No, I mean *outer* space. He's a second–hand spaceman, didn't you know? He really went there once, in a rocket. But they would never let him go again because he quarrelled so much with the other astronauts."

"Who told you that?" asked Miss Gilhoolie laughing. "Dougal McDougal?"

"No. Everyone knows. It's really true!"

"Poor Mr Jones!"

"Poor Mr Jones!" exclaimed Dougal McDougal, overhearing as Simon and the new teacher came up to the group of cockatoo admirers who had collected in the playing field. "Poor Mr Jones! I thought you were on *our* side!"

"I am not on any side," said Miss Gilhoolie

with dignity. "I am simply here to do my best! Now then Simon, where is this wonderful birthday present?"

Simon forgot the problem of ever pleasing Mr Bang Bang Jones, and concentrated instead on pointing out the perfections of his cockatoo, clearly visible as a small white dot.

"If it *is* a cockatoo!" said Dougal McDougal. "I didn't like to say so yesterday but it doesn't look much like one to me. I thought they were enormous with beaks as big as bananas."

"That's toucans," said Miss Gilhoolie laughing, while Madeline Brown commented, "It was clever of your Gran to get you binoculars too."

"Was it?"

"Of course. With them you can see her easily from the playground."

"See Gran?"

"See your cockatoo!"

"Oh," said Simon, wishing he had thought of that.

"Madeline Brown is very brainy," he

remarked gloomily to Dougal that lunchtime.

"Not compared to me she isn't."

"Compared to me she is!"

"Oh well," began Dougal McDougal cheerfully, "compared to you . . . Oh, never mind!"

"Never mind what?"

"Nothing," said Dougal, kindly changing the subject. "I tell you what, Old Bang Bang doesn't think much of Miss Gilhoolie, does he?"

"No," agreed Simon. "And she won't buy his books. I heard her telling him so."

"He wouldn't like that," pondered Dougal McDougal.

Simon Percy's diary. Wednesday, 10th September

We were talking about hobbies this morning. Madeline Brown told Miss Gilhoolie that hers was theoretical parachute jumping, and Dougal McDougal said his was getting away from his sisters, and Miss Gilhoolie said, And what about you Simon? And I said would you mind if I called my cockatoo after you Miss Gilhoolie only have you got another name because I don't think Leatherbottom sounds right for a cockatoo.

What about Featherbottom then? asked Dougal McDougal nearly dead with laughing but Miss Gilhoolie said, Thank you Simon you are very kind and my other name is Guinevere.

But she couldn't stop laughing at Dougal.

Guinevere my cockatoo.

We have got a caretaker now at Pudding Bag School. Dougal McDougal says we must have had one before but nobody ever saw him. But everyone sees Mr Bedwig. He works very hard. Already he has caught Dougal McDougal eating his dinner on the bike shed roof and mended the radiators and polished the doorknobs and got up all the chewing gum that was stuck to the playground.

"And any more that I find will go to the police for genetic fingerprinting," Mr Bedwig had announced when the last piece was removed, "and whoever spat it out will get What For From Me! And you can get down from that roof Bonnie Prince Charlie. I'm having none of that."

"How did you know I was up here?"

asked Dougal, sensibly realising that he had met his match at last, and scrambling hurriedly down.

"Look at you, all over green muck!" scolded Mr Bedwig, handing him a duster to dust himself down. "How did I know you were up there? I have been a caretaker since the year dot, and I know your sort with that red hair. My family were caretakers in the ark and you won't pull much over me young man. And who is your friend?" asked Mr Bedwig. "He is keeping very quiet which I always put down to brains."

"Oh him!" said Dougal McDougal, looking at Simon in astonishment at this reference to brains. "He is Simon Percy but we call him Simple Simon."

"Percy is a good old name and he doesn't look simple to me," said Mr Bedwig. "Simple Simon indeed!" and he winked at Simon.

Mr Bedwig is fantastic and he clears up sick so nicely. He calls it sorting out a little matter and does it with sawdust and a shovel and a mop. Much better than last year when the teachers used to shout VOLUNTEERS TO CLEAN IT UP and then go and look out of the window while the volunteers did it with paper towels. Miss Gilhoolie says I have written enough on this subject.

Simon was having a problem with Miss Gilhoolie's name. All too often it came out as Leatherbottom.

"It's your fault," he said crossly to Dougal McDougal. "Why did you tell me she was called Miss Leatherbottom?"

Dougal could never resist a joke, old or new, and who knew how many Miss Leatherbottoms Simon might be persuaded to believe in?

"I suppose I must have mixed her up with the other new teacher," he told Simon solemnly.

Simon believed in *another* Miss Leatherbottom with no difficulty at all! What was more he sought her out. She was a large and bad tempered woman, and not at all pleased to discover Simon peering at her through her classroom door with no explanation except that he had come to see if she was the real Miss Leatherbottom.

"Why ever should you ask such a silly question?" she demanded, and Simon could see her point. She certainly had a very leathery look about her, and he had no reason to suppose she was not the same all over.

"I don't know, Miss Leatherbottom," he said meekly, and this reply was taken as extreme cheek and he found himself being marched off to Miss Gilhoolie and complained about. Miss Gilhoolie, who was getting quite tired of hearing about leather bottoms herself, said, "Really Simon! I think you ought to stop believing everything Dougal McDougal tells you!"

Then Simon went out into the playground and picked a fight with Dougal McDougal.

CHAPTER THREE

The fight between Simon Percy and Dougal McDougal only ended when Mr Bedwig emerged suddenly from the boiler house and plucked them apart.

"I have never seen the like!" he exclaimed, regarding them both with great indignation. "Dougal McDougal, you should be ashamed! Look at the state of him, and not a mark on you!"

"But he . . ."

"Not a word!" interrupted Mr Bedwig, cutting off Dougal's protests at once. "The bell has long gone so into class with you and no argy-bargy! Simon Percy, straight to the cloakroom and get that blood off before you give someone a turn! And brush yourself down while you're about it. There is half the playground stuck on the back of that jumper of yours! Now hop it!"

Simon hopped it without a word, but Dougal McDougal, outraged at being seized on the point of victory and blamed for a fight he had not begun, had to be escorted protesting from the battlefield and personally delivered to a most unsympathetic Miss Gilhoolie.

"Fighting!" she exclaimed crossly. "I thought you and Simon were friends Dougal! Poor Simon!"

She also refused to listen to any kind of argy-bargy.

In the cloakroom Simon wiped his nose, brushed down his clothes, and washed away the dirt and tears that Mr Bedwig had so kindly mistaken for blood. Then he located a hiding place and crawled inside and was discovered almost at once by Mr Bedwig.

"Out of that young Simon!" he ordered, but not unkindly. "Chop chop! Toot sweet! There's never been a battle won yet from under a heap of coats! That there Dougal McDougal the red–headed Scot has caught it hot and strong from your Miss Gilhoolie!"

"Has he?"

"She is a proper cracker, your new teacher," continued Mr Bedwig, as Simon began to emerge into daylight again. "A proper cracker! I shall get her desk stopped wobbling tonight. It is dropping to bits and her blackboard could do with a coat of paint. Now then, quick march! She is worrying about you!"

There was obviously no use in protesting. Before he knew it Simon was back in the classroom. There he had to stand up while Dougal said, "Sorry I hit you and sorry I told you the other new teacher was called Miss Leatherbottom. It was a joke. I didn't know you would go and call her it. But you hit me first so I don't see why *I* am getting all the blame!"

"That's enough!" interrupted Miss Gilhoolie hastily, before the fight could begin again. "Sit down and I'll read us a story to cheer us all up."

"Huh!" said Dougal bitterly, but he sat down anyway.

Miss Gilhoolie gave him a hard look over the top of her book but made no comment.

"Last One In the Playground!" she read aloud. "A ghost story!"

"You thumped me first and I am getting all the blame!" whispered Dougal to Simon as soon as Miss Gilhoolie was well under way. "You ought to say sorry for making me say sorry!"

"You started it!" Simon whispered back. "You got *me* in trouble. Telling me that other new teacher was called Miss Leatherbottom! And you said Miss Gilhoolie was called Miss Leatherbottom too!"

Miss Gilhoolie paused in her reading to glare at them both.

"It was a trick! It was meant to be funny." hissed Dougal the moment she looked down again.

"They both HATE being called Miss Leatherbottom!" replied Simon, not very quietly, and then Miss Gilhoolie banged her book shut and said she was not reading to such rude, ungrateful people any longer.

"You can write up your diaries until the bell goes!" she ordered. "And no wailing! Or it will be worse. It will be table tests!"

The horrible coolness between Simon and Dougal lasted all Friday morning and right through lunch. Simon was so upset that he had not even the heart to go out and wave to Guinevere. Instead he took refuge in the Lost Property cupboard and was routed out almost at once by Mr Bedwig.

"I don't know what you are thinking of!" exclaimed Mr Bedwig. "You are letting down the family name and no mistake! The Percys in the past never hid in cupboards! Come out of all that muck before you catch something nasty. There's places in this school worse than the ark on the thirty–ninth day! I wasn't sent a moment too soon!"

"Were you sent?" asked Simon, as he crawled obediently out. "Who by?"

"Agency," said Mr Bedwig, tutting with disgust as he turned over a pile of mouldering plimsolls. "Knights in armour since the court of King Arthur, the Percys have been."

"Oh," said Simon.

"And you in a cupboard!"

"*What* agency?" asked Simon, suddenly remembering the advertisement he had read in the sweet shop on the first day of term. "Not the *Best In All The World* one?"

"And why not?"

"I wonder if that's where Gran got my cockatoo from."

"If I were you I would get out into the sunshine young Percy, and stop wondering quite so much."

"What *was* the ark like on the thirty–ninth day?"

"According to my dad it was far from sparkling," said Mr Bedwig, shepherding Simon towards the door. "Far from! Damp was not the word for it! And no pumps either! It was bail or to the bottom! And you think *you* have problems! Out you go and give that cockatoo a wave before the bell goes!"

Simon went, and on the doorstep almost fell over Madeline Brown who was sitting with her chin on her knees and an expression of great concentration on her face.

"It would be terrible if old Bang Bang got rid of Miss Gilhoolie," she said.

Simon was so startled that he nearly collapsed. "Terrible," repeated Madeline, winding her plaits round her fists and pulling as hard as she could. "Wouldn't it?"

"How could he?" asked Simon in amazement.

"He's been staring out of his window all this time," said Madeline, ignoring Simon's question. "She's been out here teaching Dougal the Highland Fling and he's been watching with a face like . . . a face like . . .

well, even worse than it usually is, and I suddenly thought . . ."

"What?"

"How *terrible* it would be if he got rid of Miss Gilhoolie," said Madeline.

The Highland Fling must have had a softening effect on Dougal McDougal because at the end of afternoon school he dashed back into the classroom where Simon, last as usual, was getting ready to go home, and pushed a note into his hand before charging back outside again.

ALL RIGHT. PEACE. PAX. FRIENDS.

"Peace Pax Friends!" read Simon aloud, and then, needing to tell someone the good news, ran into the cloakroom where Mr Bedwig was usually to be found at that time of day.

"Peace Pax Friends! Mr Bedwig!" called Simon, rushing up and down the aisles between the coatpegs. "Mr Bedwig! Mr Bedwig! It's Peace Pax Friends!"

But there was no Mr Bedwig in the

cloakroom. Nor in the washrooms or the corridors or the rattling empty classrooms. Simon searched them all. The basement light was still shining but Mr Bedwig was not there either.

"He must have gone home," said Simon at last, and hollow with disappointment was trudging back through the echoing school when a sudden movement caught his eye. It was in his own classroom and it was Mr Bang Bang Jones.

"Ruining them!" he heard Mr Jones exclaim, stooping over a table laden with collages of Autumn leaves, Class 4b's afternoon art work and still not quite dry. "Ruining them! Gluing leaves on bits of paper! And dancing in the playground! Dancing! It will have to be stopped!"

Suddenly, like a sort of warning, Madeline's words came back to Simon.

It would be terrible if Old Bang Bang got rid of Miss Gilhoolie.

"I shall need them back for research in the very near future and they will be absolutely ruined!"

At that moment a quiet voice behind Simon remarked, "I should go home Young Percy! It is more than time," and Simon spun round and there was Mr Bedwig.

"Peace Pax Friends, isn't it?" asked Mr Bedwig. "And very nice too."

"Oh . . . !" began Simon.

"Kingdoms have been signed away for less! Now off you go!"

Simon wanted to say, "Who told you it was Peace Pax Friends?" He wanted to say, "Look at Mr Jones! Wouldn't it be awful if Mr Jones got rid of Miss Gilhoolie?" And he would like to have asked more about the sweet shop agency, and the Percys from the past, and conditions in the ark, and Mr Bedwig's opinions on hot air ballooning holidays, and the possibilities of birthday wishes ever coming true. But he said, "Yes Mr Bedwig."

And went home.

On his way down Pudding Bag Lane Simon stopped to have a look at the sweet shop, and found it as discouragingly closed as ever. He could not remember ever having seen it any other way.

"It opens when necessary," said Gran, when he mentioned it that night. "What were you wanting?"

"Nothing particular," said Simon.

"Well then," said Gran.

"But is that where you got Guinevere from?"

"Yes indeed," agreed Gran brightly. "I ordered her at the beginning of summer as a matter of fact. I told them what a dreadful time you were having at school and they suggested that she would be just the thing."

Guinevere, who had been perched on the curtain rail listening to this conversation, flew down to the tea table and landed beside Simon's plate.

"Just the thing," repeated Gran with satisfaction. "Dear Guinevere!"

"I wish I could take her to school on Monday," said Simon. "Then Miss Gilhoolie would see her properly. Do you think I could? Her cage could stand on the Interest Table. There's nothing on it yet."

"Nothing of interest?"

"Nothing at all."

"Then you must certainly take Guinevere,"
said Gran.

On Monday morning there was a surprise waiting for Class 4b.

"I came by a drop of emulsion," said Mr Bedwig.

The classroom walls, previously a hideous and scabby peppermint green, were painted sunshine yellow. The ceiling was sky blue. Around the blackboard and along the bottoms of the window frames were brilliant roses and carnations, scarlet and pink, picked out in gold. Patches of broken plaster on walls and ceiling had been transformed into an assortment of green and red dragons.

"Mr Bedwig!" exclaimed Miss Gilhoolie. "You are a genius!"

"It is a knack I picked up from my old dad," said Mr Bedwig. "There was nothing he couldn't do with a paintbrush and a pot of bright red."

"It is absolutely wonderful," said Miss Gilhoolie, who was dressed in bright red herself that morning, very short and shimmering and with diamonds in her hair. "Exquisite! Goodness Simon!" She stopped when she caught sight of some white feathers. "Whatever have you there?"

"It's Guinevere," said Simon shyly. "For the Interest Table."

"She is the perfect finishing touch," said Miss Gilhoolie, smiling broadly. "But now to work, to work! Mathematics, Class 4b! Volume and Capacity! It is on the National Curriculum so we must try and take it seriously . . ."

This sounded quite worrying but Class 4b soon discovered that Volume and Capacity, with real sand and water to measure, was nothing like any Maths lesson ever taught by Mr Bang Bang Jones. They were completely engrossed when the door flew open and the headmaster erupted into the room.

"WHAT is going on in this class?" roared Mr Bang Bang Jones. "What? What! Kindly explain Young Miss!"

"It is Volume and Capacity, dear Mr Jones," said Miss Gilhoolie soothingly.

"Volume and Capacity!" repeated Mr Jones, not ceasing to roar. "It is Buckets and Spades!"

"Well, naturally..."

"There are shells in the sand and goldfish in the water!"

"To add interest and discourage spillage."

"I must say also that I consider you most unfittingly dressed..."

"Oh Mr Jones," protested Miss Gilhoolie, smiling. "All Paris knows that diamonds go with anything!"

"AND WHAT HAS HAPPENED TO THESE CLASSROOM WALLS?" This was the last straw.

"I came by a drop of emulsion," said Mr Bedwig from behind.

"Outrageous!" spluttered Mr Bang Bang Jones, half choking with temper. "They must instantly be repainted Educational Green!"

"That cannot be," said Mr Bedwig, much to Class 4b's relief. "That cannot be as I have used up the last of the Decorating Allocation for the next twenty years. Should you wish me to hand in my notice I will do it at once, but I must warn you that the radiator in your study is giving out bangs and blue flashes and the electrician will not touch it on account of his Insurance and so there is *Only Me.*"

Mr Bang Bang Jones glared at Mr Bedwig with the helpless fury of the utterly vanquished, and then all of a sudden his eye was caught by a movement on the Interest Table.

CHAPTER FOUR

"Simon dear, do not cry like that!" begged Miss Gilhoolie. "Or at least, not quite so loudly. Mr Bedwig and I cannot think when you howl! Guinevere is only confiscated, remember! She is not gone for good! Somebody find his diary for him please! It will give him something to occupy his mind. Good girl Madeline! And he'll need a pen."

"I've given him a pencil," said Madeline. "Because of the tears."

Mr Jones has confiscated Guinevere, wrote Simon.

"You had better not do any more until the paper gets less damp," said Madeline, and she took his diary away and draped it over a radiator to dry out. It took quite a long time, and during that time Miss Gilhoolie and Mr

Bedwig tried in vain to recover Guinevere.

Miss Gilhoolie went first and she left the door propped open behind her so that she could keep an eye on Simon's tears. This meant that Class 4b, sitting as still as mice, could hear all that went on in the corridor outside the headmaster's door.

"Mr Jones, Sir," called Miss Gilhoolie, having knocked for some time and received no answer. "It is I, Miss Gilhoolie. I must explain that I am entirely to blame. It was I who encouraged the children to bring their treasures to the Interest Table. Do let me come in and apologize."

"Too late Miss!" snapped Old Bang Bang. "Class 4b are very important research material! I will not have them distracted by parrots!"

After that Mr Bedwig had a go, clumping up to call through the keyhole that there was a burst water main in the playing field that the headmaster really ought to inspect.

"I am a professional not a plumber!"

shouted Mr Jones through the locked office door.

Then Miss Gilhoolie tried again, saying she had reconsidered her previous decision about buying the headmaster's lovely books, and asking if she could come in and arrange to purchase half a dozen of all three volumes and any past works as well.

"I have taken note of your order and will have the balance deducted from your salary," replied Old Bang Bang immediately. "You may go."

So then Mr Bedwig told him the National Press seemed to be at the door and what should he tell them about rumours of a possible knighthood?

That did not work either.

"Well," said Miss Gilhoolie, "I suppose it will have to be the diamonds," and she pushed them under the door in an envelope labelled:

RANSOM. RETURN THE COCKATOO.

and she was very cross when old Bang Bang

said they were gaudy fakes and pushed them back.

Dougal McDougal suggested that Mr Bedwig turn up the heating so high that Old Bang Bang would be cooked into giving in but Madeline Brown said straight away, "Guinevere would be cooked too."

So that was not tried, and Mr Bedwig would not let anyone set off the fire alarm either.

"Let me see if he would care for some lunch," said Miss Gilhoolie.

She closed the door behind her and was gone for some time, but eventually returned looking quite pink and indignant and said, "No good Simon, the wretched creature has brought sandwiches! I am afraid you will have to wait until four o'clock. I cannot try again. He simply won't listen to reason."

There followed a long and anxious afternoon, but towards the end Mr Bedwig cheered them up tremendously by coming in to announce that Guinevere was perfectly safe and well.

"How do you know?" asked Simon.

"Seen her," said Mr Bedwig. "Quite by chance as I was up a ladder cleaning the study windows. Which were – by the way – flung open with great recklessness just as I reached the top pane and I shan't forget *that* in a hurry. No telling where I would be if I hadn't happened to land head first on a passing very strong cat! I am going out now for a tin of best salmon and then there is a sizable hole in the playground to be filled in! Do not look like that Simon Percy. It is nothing compared to the troubles they had during the Flood."

At four o'clock Simon Percy was allowed into the office to collect the confiscated Guinevere. Here he had to listen to a lot of noise about hard work and science and who might be the original Pudding Bag of Pudding Bag School. At the bit about the original Pudding Bag something inside him stirred, and Simon Percy, descendant of King Arthur's knights, found the courage to attack.

"You ought to say sorry to Mr Bedwig!" squeaked Simon Percy.

"WHAT DID YOU SAY?"

"I said you ought to say sorry to Mr Bedwig," repeated Simon, nearly dead with fright. "You bumped him off his ladder and he might have been hurt very badly if it wasn't for a passing very strong cat."

There was a long, long silence, during which time Mr Jones changed colour from white to red and then to purplish black before slowly fading back to white, and Simon stood expecting the end of the world.

The end of the world did not come, and Simon, as if from a long way off, heard his own voice saying, in a sort of astonished bleat. "And I don't like being called the original Pudding Bag!"

Mr Jones stared at him, clearly thinking that Simon had gone quite mad.

"And you'd better have been kind to Guinevere!" said the same far away voice. And then Simon seized Guinevere and ran out of the door and he did not stop running until he was out of school and across the playground and halfway down Pudding Bag Lane. Dougal McDougal and Madeline

Brown, who had been listening at the keyhole, caught up with him there.

"Tell us what happened," begged Dougal McDougal, quite out of breath. "We couldn't hear anything but strange sorts of squeaks. We were going to rush in if you started screaming."

"Tell us first if Guinevere's all right," said Madeline calmly.

"She's quite all right," said Simon, displaying Guinevere in her cage. "Did Mr Jones chase after me?"

"No."

"I thought he might."

"Was he very cross?"

"He was when I cheeked him."

"You *cheeked* him?" repeated Dougal.

"Tell us from the beginning," urged Madeline Brown.

"I went in," said Simon, "and he was writing . . ."

"More books?"

"No. In a big black file."

"Black?"

"Yes, with a label on the front . . ."

"What did it say?" demanded Dougal, hungry for every detail.

"I couldn't read it all. He covered it up almost straight away. EVIDENCE FOR THE DISMISS something, it began. And then he told me a lot of stuff about Hard Work and Science and if I ever took Guinevere in again he wouldn't hesitate to confiscate her once more and then he started on about me being the original Pudding Bag . . . don't laugh!"

"We never do laugh!" said Madeline indignantly.

"Sorry. And then I got a very strange feeling, very strange, like when you have a temperature and can't think straight and I tried to shout but it came out a squeak and I told him he should say sorry to Mr Bedwig. And a bit later on I told him he'd better have been kind to Guinevere and then I came away." Simon couldn't believe he was talking about himself.

"You did exactly what I would have done," said Dougal McDougal in the tone of one who can give no higher praise.

"Evidence for the dismiss?" said Madeline

thoughtfully. "Evidence for the dismiss? I don't like the sound of that very much. I don't like the sound of it at all! I hope Miss Gilhoolie's going to be all right."

But Simon was crooning to Guinevere, and Dougal was outlining all the other things that somebody ought to say to Mr Bang Bang Jones and nobody took any notice of Madeline.

CHAPTER FIVE

That night Simon dreamed of school, and even in his dreams Mr Jones was still talking.

"Original Pudding Bag," said the dream Mr Jones. "Dratted parrot! I have brought sandwiches, sandwiches, thank you Miss! And I do not like what is happening to Class 4b! They will be changed beyond recognition and useless for my research! Impertinent Young Woman! She will have to go!"

"No, no!" protested Simon, who while he slept was once again an unhappy visitor to Old Bang Bang's study.

"Eighteen volumes, she had ordered," mused the dream Mr Jones (not seeming to notice what Simon had just noticed, that the dream Simon Percy was clothed entirely in paper, pages from his diary). "Eighteen volumes! Enormous profits! But nevertheless she will have to go!"

Oh where is my school uniform? dreamed Simon in despair, and not daring to move in case the paper clothes disintegrated around him. Oh where is it? He will notice in a minute!

But the dream Mr Jones had other things on his mind.

"I shall put it to the Governors that a mistake has been made. She should never have been appointed. I shall present the evidence for the dismiss—"

With a jump Simon was suddenly awake.

"—al of Guinevere Gilhoolie," said the dream Mr Jones, obviously unaware that Simon was no longer sleeping.

Simon lay, frozen with terror, staring into the dark, certain he had not dreamed that voice, straining his ears for the slightest whisper, dreading to hear it.

No sound came.

Gradually his heart stopped pounding so loudly. He allowed himself to breathe more naturally, and at last began to drift back into sleep.

"Dratted parrot!" hissed Mr Jones, right into Simon's ear.

All at once the bedroom light was switched on, and there was Gran standing in the doorway, and Guinevere blinking at the sudden brightness and ruffling her feathers, and no one else except Simon sitting stiff and straight in bed with a ringing in his ears and a tightness in his throat, and a memory of terrible shrieking.

"Simon!" exclaimed Gran. "Simon!"

It came to Simon then that the shrieks had been his own.

"Such awful screaming! Whatever were you dreaming?"

"I dreamed about school," explained Simon, beginning to gabble as he woke up more and more. "About Mr Jones. I was in his office and I couldn't find my uniform. I was wearing my diary and I thought he would read it and he was talking and talking and then I woke up, wide properly awake just like I am now and he was still talking. In my room. Talking. On my pillow. Right in my ear. Right in my ear!"

"You were asleep."

"Right in my *ear*! I almost felt him."

"You were asleep," repeated Gran again. "You were asleep when I came in. You didn't know you were screaming. It was just a dream Simon. You're still half asleep now."

"I'm not," grumbled Simon, already asleep.

Gran sat with him for a while, idly patting the bump under the quilt that was Simon's feet, and watching Guinevere as she preened and sleeked her feathers into place. The room was filled with a lovely quiet.

"He'll do now," said Gran after a while, and switching off the light went sleepily back to bed.

"She is ruining that class!" grumbled Mr Jones crossly. "Already they are changed! They will be useless for research! She will *have* to go. My work must be considered. The eagerly awaited sequel to PRACTICAL PUNISHMENTS . . ."

Simon was wide awake. By means of a small miracle, he was managing not to faint.

"SILENCE AT ALL COSTS

THE ULTIMATE GUIDE TO THE
CONTROL OF ALIEN LIFE FORMS
Author: Sir B. B. Jones."

I am *completely* awake, thought Simon wildly, as he cowered under his quilt.

"Sandwiches," continued Mr Jones. "I have brought sandwiches thank you Miss! Simon Percy, the original Pudd . . ."

All at once Simon could bear it no longer. He threw back the quilt, turned on the light and plumped indignantly up in his bed.

"I *don't like* being called . . ." he began furiously.

". . . ing Bag," said Guinevere.

The relief and astonishment was like a sudden burst of stars.

"Dratted parrot!" said Guinevere again, in exactly Old Bang Bang's voice and Simon found himself laughing. He could not help it. He was so glad to find himself safe in bed, safe in *pyjamas*, and to know that it had been Guinevere all along, not old Bang Bang Jones conjured terribly into the night. Brilliant, wonderful Guinevere! thought Simon. Without doubt she must be the most intelligent cockatoo in the world!

"Look at that radiator!" continued Guinevere, completely unaware of the shock she had given her owner. "Bangs and blue flashes! That idiotic caretaker has wired it to the mains!"

Simon chuckled happily.

"I *must* collect evidence! Evidence, evidence! Evidence for the dismissal of Guinevere Gilhoolie."

There won't be any to collect, thought Simon. Miss Gilhoolie is perfect!

"And then to resume my Great Work. SILENCE AT ALL COSTS! Extravagantly researched! Extravagantly researched on Class 4b!"

It was only Guinevere. Simon knew it was only Guinevere, but nevertheless, he shuddered.

From the diary of Simon Percy. Tuesday, 12th September

You won't believe what happened yesterday I said to Dougal McDougal and Madeline Brown and I

told them about Guinevere in the night and I
really thought they wouldn't believe it and would
just laugh. But they didn't.

To recapitulate, said Madeline Brown, who is
very clever. Guinevere has overheard his secret
plan. He does not like Miss Gilhoolie. He thinks
she is spoiling us and he is collecting evidence so
that he can make the Governors get rid of her.
And then he will take Class 4b back again. And
he will use us to research his horrible new book
which is called SILENCE AT ALL COSTS. It
sounds ten million times worse than PRAC-
TICAL PUNISHMENTS. This is very serious.

It is Old Bang Bang who ought to be got rid of,
not Miss Gilhoolie said Dougal. I wish he had
stayed in Outer Space. It's a pity he ever came
back. Simon Percy, do you have to write every-
thing down in that diary of yours?

Yes I do.

For as long as he could remember Simon had
had a feeling that he was missing something.
He had never quite been able to keep up with
the world around him. His days had been
muddled and his nights harassed. He had

never quite grasped what he was there for. With the arrival of his diary he suddenly understood. He was the one who wrote it all down. Nothing need ever pass him by again.

Madeline and Dougal watched as he sat in the playground on a broken bike-stand and brought them up to date.

"I can see why he likes to do it," admitted Madeline.

"I can't," said Dougal. "I could never be bothered. Hello! What's everyone looking at over there?"

A crowd had collected at the gates around Samantha Freebody, also a member of Class 4b.

"What is it?" asked Madeline, seeing Samantha's anxious face.

"It's a letter of complaint from my mum," said Samantha, passing a sheet of blue writing paper to Madeline. "Read it!"

Dear Miss Gilhoolie, said Samantha's letter *We have been up all night with our Samantha on account of the ghost stories she has been listening to in class. Also she has been over excited since the start of term about one thing and another and now she is pestering for diamonds. Kindly do not put ideas in our Samantha's head.*

"It's not my fault," said Samantha, sniffing wetly. "Fancy having to give poor Miss Gilhoolie that when she's been so kind! Lending me her diamond necklace when I cut both knees and making the dinner ladies stop giving me gravy and . . ."

"You mustn't give that note to Miss Gilhoolie!" interrupted Madeline decisively. "You must eat it at once Samantha! Notes from home get put in the register and that means Old Bang Bang will see it and it is exactly the kind of evidence he wants. Eat it at once. It is only short!"

Samantha saw immediately that this was the only thing to do, the sooner the better. She only just managed to gulp down the final fragments as Miss Gilhoolie appeared among them.

"Such a lovely windy day," said Miss Gilhoolie cheerfully. "And as you have all worked so hard lately I thought we would devote the morning to kite–making . . . Mr Bedwig has popped out to the sweet shop to collect what we shall need . . ."

The bell rang as at least a dozen people beseiged her with descriptions of the hopelessness of ever trying to obtain anything at all from the Pudding Bag Lane sweet shop.

"Line up! Line up and stop worrying!" said Miss Gilhoolie, ignoring them all, and later there was great astonishment in Class 4b when Mr Bedwig arrived laden at the classroom door. He had bought coloured paper, balls of string, glue, bamboo and a large bag of pearly fresh mushrooms which he explained were for his lunch.

"It opens when necessary," he remarked placidly, exactly as Simon's Gran had done. "Lovely mushrooms! Fresh as fresh. I shall do them in butter with a sprinkle of nutmeg." The smell of them frying drifted into the classroom as the kite–making got under way.

"We will have to have a mushrooming expedition of our own," remarked Miss Gilhoolie. "Write it down in your diary

Simon and remind me next week!"

Not even the arrival of Miss Gilhoolie's books spoilt that happy morning.

They came by lorry in three big boxes, recorded Simon in his diary.

Push them under the Interest Table said Miss Gilhoolie, and we will try and forget about them, but when Mr Jones came in to complain about the mushroom smell he noticed them straight away. I trust they are not my books, he said. Yes indeed, said Miss Gilhoolie. They will be safe under there. Do you not care for mushrooms Mr Jones? The smell is coming up from a knothole in the floorboards and we are all enjoying it very much. However if you find it too tantalizing I could arrange your books over the knothole. What do you think?

Mr Jones marched out of the room then but he came back almost straight away and said KITE–MAKING in a very cross voice.

Quite right said Miss Gilhoolie.

The kites worked beautifully.

"Art, design and technology, observation

of weather conditions, physical education and local space exploration," said Miss Gilhoolie in reply to Mr Jones' rude comments about time wasting.

"There will be complaints from parents if this sort of thing goes on!" snapped Mr Jones.

"There have been none so far," replied Miss Gilhoolie, and Samanatha, overhearing, swallowed thankfully.

Madeline called a class meeting after school last night, wrote Simon in his diary the next day. *So now everyone knows what Guinevere heard while she was being confiscated. And everyone is going to be very careful and show notes from parents to Madeline before they hand them in.*

You can always tell Miss Gilhoolie what the notes were about if you are feeling guilty, said Madeline. It is the written evidence that is dangerous.

Miss Gilhoolie says if we do Maths all morning then this afternoon we can go conkering in the park.

Old Bang Bang won't think much of conkering said Dougal McDougal.

Well then we will call it a nature walk said Miss Gilhoolie, and do not call him that again please Dougal.

He doesn't like nature walks, said Dougal.

A scientific expedition then, said Miss Gilhoolie.

He'll want to come, said Dougal.

Well then we will just sneak off, said Miss Gilhoolie getting a bit cross with Dougal. I cannot be worrying about what will upset Mr Jones all the time. There is a trapdoor Mr Bedwig has very kindly made under my desk leading straight to the basement and a tunnel out from the basement where the coke used to come in. We will get out that way and he will never know we are gone.

He will if he comes in, said Dougal.

We will barricade the door from the inside with his books, said Miss Gilhoolie. Might as well make some use of them.

Awful if he finds out, said Dougal.

Dougal McDougal do you want to go out through the basement tunnel (which I hear Mr Bedwig has lit with old Christmas tree lights) and go conkering in the park, or not? asked Miss Gilhoolie, so Dougal shut up and we are going *straight after lunch. Miss Gilhoolie says she knows a brilliant tree. And she says we can take the kites for when we have got enough conkers and on the way we are going to stop at my house for Guinevere and Gran.*

School never used to be like this, wrote Simon.

CHAPTER SIX

"Is that homework, Simon?" asked Gran one evening.

"It's my diary," said Simon.

Simon's diary was now quite famous in Pudding Bag School. Rumours of it even reached as far as the headmaster's study (which would have alarmed Simon very much if he had known because the accounts concerning Mr Bang Bang Jones, although true, were far from flattering).

At different times favoured friends had been allowed private glimpses. Both Miss Gilhoolie and Mr Bedwig had read of the loss of Simon's parents when he was six weeks old. It had seemed to Simon very important that this should be recorded, and Miss Gilhoolie, when consulted, had agreed.

"Even though it was ages ago?" Simon had asked anxiously.

"You could not possibly have written it at the time," pointed out Miss Gilhoolie.

Simon's account of the fateful box of teabags on which the competition had appeared, the hot air ballooning holiday in the foothills of the Himalayas that had resulted, and the postcard that had arrived three years later, moved Miss Gilhoolie to tears.

"Show Mr Bedwig," she said at last. "Perhaps he will be able to think of something."

Mr Bedwig wrestled in silence with Simon's handwriting (which looked exactly like a train of rolled–up hedgehogs), and then cleared his throat and said, "Well."

"Well what?" asked Simon.

"Well I shall have to have a think."

"Have you got an idea then?" asked Simon eagerly.

"I can't say I have just at the moment."

"Oh," said Simon.

"Ten years is a long time."

"I know." Simon had been certain that if anyone could help it would be Mr Bedwig and he had to struggle hard not to show the disappointment he was feeling. "I know it is."

"I could ask around. Get some advice."

"Never mind."

"Come on Young Percy! Never say d—" Mr Bedwig stopped and hastily changed the subject.

"I am planning a proper wopper of a bonfire on that spot where they put the burnt out mobile classroom you had," he told Simon confidentially. "Him Up There knows nothing about it, he has kept well out of my way since the drains went back on us. What do you say to having a real old fashioned bonfire night and you can light the touch paper?"

"Thank you very much," said Simon.

"That's a good lad," said Mr Bedwig. "I know nothing about the Himalayas but perhaps it is just that they are finding it a long way back."

"Your trapdoor under Miss Gilhoolie's desk has been very useful." Simon, sorry to see Mr Bedwig looking so downcast, tried anxiously to cheer him up by changing the subject.

"Has it now?"

"We've been conkering," said Simon. "Roller skating, apple picking and we went to the cinema with the apple picking money, and today we're going on a mushroom hunt."

"And why not?" said Mr Bedwig. "You are only young once. You mind what you pick this afternoon though, you don't want any more letters of complaint to dispose of."

Simon completely agreed. Letters of complaint, and Madeline Brown's insistence as to the only safe way of disposing of them, were becoming rather a problem.

"We cannot afford to be careless," said Madeline. "Mr Jones is getting worse than ever. He searches for evidence all the time. Simon and I have watched him after school from Simon's bedroom window, going through the bins. If your parents *must* write letters try and make them do it on rice paper. You can buy it at the bakers."

The mushroom hunt led to a major problem in evidence disposal.

Monday, 24th September

Everyone in Class 4b has stomach ache and it is Dougal McDougal's fault. It is because of the toadstool he found on the mushroom hunt.

Do not pick that toadstool Dougal, Miss Gilhoolie told him. It is not the sort of thing we want on the Interest Table. It is Highly Dangerous. There is enough poison in that to put you to sleep for a fortnight.

She made Dougal put it down and he did. But then he had an idea and he thought it would be nice to have two days peace from his seven sisters. So he went back and hid it in his pocket.

He took it home and squeezed out the juice.

He made seven cups of toadstool juice coffee, one for each of his sisters and he said they thought they had got him trained at last.

His sisters are a big nuisance but when they had drunk the coffee Dougal suddenly got worried and he told his mum what he had done and his mum said he was a very naughty boy and now his sisters would have to be stomach pumped.

This happened.

One of Dougal's sisters forgot to drink her coffee and so escaped but the other six and Dougal's mum wrote very long letters of complaint to Miss Gilhoolie. Fifty–three pages.

Class effort, said Madeline Brown when she saw them. Two pages each and the extra one for Dougal.

A lot of people are saying we cannot go on like this.

"If Dougal would like to choose two friends to help him barricade the door," began Miss Gilhoolie the following day, "We will drop in on Mr Bedwig and do some cooking. It is too wet to go out but there is a lovely fire going in the boiler and I will show you how to make toffee-apples."

Madeline Brown sighed, but she had to do something. She put up her hand and said, "Please Miss Gilhoolie, couldn't we just do some nice, quiet National Curriculum instead?"

Class 4b, to whom toffee-apple–making

had seemed the perfect way of spending a wet October afternoon, stared at Madeline in amazement and Miss Gilhoolie, who had already opened the trapdoor and was busy unpacking bags of apples and butter and sugar, said faintly, "Madeline dear! Are you ill?"

"I just thought," said Madeline, "that perhaps making toffee-apples might not be such a good idea . . . the stickiness . . ."

People were looking at her as if she had gone mad. ". . . the stickiness and toffee on clothes," went on Madeline, persevering despite the awful looks she was being given, "and supposing someone fell into the boiler or turned out to be allergic to apples . . ."

Light was beginning to dawn on Class 4b and there was a general murmur of agreement. Dougal McDougal, who had been on his feet staring at Madeline in horror slowly sat back down again.

"It might lead to anything," continued Madeline. "Letters of complaint . . ."

"Letters of complaint!" repeated Miss Gilhoolie indignantly. "My dear Madeline I must tell you that in my whole career of teaching I have never had a single letter of complaint! Dougal McDougal I cannot think what you find so amusing!"

"I wasn't laughing," said Dougal. "It was a hiccup. I have had a lot of hiccups lately. I think it is something I ate."

This remark caused much sniggering.

"I consider that very rude Dougal," said Miss Gilhoolie severely. "Madeline, your objections are ridiculous! And the rest of you are behaving like sheep! Dougal McDougal, did you bleat?"

"Yes," said Dougal noticing unhappily that Miss Gilhoolie was now repacking the toffee-apple ingredients at lightning speed. "Before I thought. I am sorry Miss Gilhoolie. Let's go and make toffee-apples like you said. I bet you don't get any letters of complaint."

"I bet I don't too," said Miss Gilhoolie very crossly, as she slammed the trapdoor shut. "Get out pencils and rough books Class 4b. Simon Percy, put that diary away! The next few hours will not be worth recording."

"We should have made those toffee-apples," said Samuel Moon to Madeline the next morning. Samuel was not usually the sort of person to grumble, and Madeline stared at him in surprise. "My mum's made me bring in a letter of complaint," went on Samuel. "Just because I fell asleep at tea. Look! Read it!"

Dear Madam, Samuel's letter began.
Samuel came home very tired yesterday after school. He tells me he had fractions and decimals, a spelling test, jogging on the spot, a poem to write on What Science Means To Me and they were kept in at playtime to tidy their desks. Samuel is only ten and four months and he had Bad Ears as a baby and I think this is too much.

"I am very sorry Madeline," said Samuel. "But it is only one page and I have brought a pot of marmite that I thought might help."

"But you mustn't eat *this*, Samuel," said Madeline at once. "Don't you realise it's exactly the sort of thing Old Bang Bang ought to see?"

"Is it?"

"He's looking for proof that we *don't* work, not that we do! It would be a terrible waste to eat this letter!"

"Would it?"

"You should just hand it in and see what happens."

"Happens about *what*?" demanded Old Bang Bang, pouncing suddenly between them. "Kindly explain yourselves! Happens about what?"

"Abo . . . abo . . . abo . . . abo . . ." said Samuel.

"About this letter of complaint that Samuel's mother has sent to Miss Gilhoolie," said Madeline.

"Well! Well! Well!" exclaimed Mr Jones, gleefully rubbing his hands together as he stooped to grab. "At last! At last! At last!" And he unfolded the letter with greedy haste.

Madeline watched with interest. His eyes bulged further and further as he read to the end. He did not seem pleased. He wasn't.

"Can't your wretched mother write a

better letter of complaint than this?" he shouted, screwing up the letter and thrusting it back at the unfortunate Samuel (who was still stammering "abo . . . abo . . . abo . . ."). "Put it in a bin! Put it in the bin!"

Silently Samuel did as he was told.

"He's really horrible isn't he," Samuel said to Madeline when Mr Jones was safely out of the way.

"Yes."

"And he doesn't like Miss Gilhoolie at all."

"No. At first it was because she was too cheerful and wouldn't do as he said, but now he just doesn't like her. She's not frightened of him. No wonder he wants to get rid of her."

At break that morning Miss Gilhoolie suddenly remarked. "It seemed a shame to waste those things I brought yesterday," and disappeared into the stock cupboard. She came out again holding two large trays of toffee-apples, golden and shiny with lollipop stick handles.

"Miss Gilhoolie is the best teacher in the world," said Simon Percy.

"Yes, and Old Bang Bang is a rotten pig," agreed Samuel. "Try and think of something Madeline!"

"I am trying," said Madeline.

CHAPTER SEVEN

Madeline, Dougal and Simon held a crisis meeting in Simon's bedroom. It was so small that the only way they could all fit in was by sitting in a line on the bed. Opposite them, on the table under the window, was Guinevere. She had been given a bowl of sunflower seeds and was picking through them delicately and occasionally selecting one to crack while listening to the conversation. Every now and then she looked thoughtfully at Madeline and blinked one eye.

Oh Guinevere! thought Madeline, and tried very hard to avoid looking at her as she said, "It is Mr Jones or Miss Gilhoolie, plain as plain. One of them will have to go and I hope it won't be Miss Gilhoolie. I just wish I knew how Old Bang Bang was getting on with his evidence."

Simon knew what was coming then, even before Dougal put it into words.

"Guinevere could find out," he said.

"Only if Simon really doesn't mind," said Madeline.

Simon gulped because he minded very much, but he said bravely, "He didn't hurt her last time, did he? Or scare her?"

Guinevere shook her feathers and looked scornfully down her beak at the suggestion that she might be frightened of such an earth-bound creature as Mr Bang Bang Jones.

" 'Course he didn't scare her!" said Dougal robustly. "He didn't even scare *you*! You cheeked him, remember!"

"Yes," agreed Simon uncertainly, and he couldn't help wondering if the Percys in the past (whose behaviour Mr Bedwig so highly recommended) ever trembled as he was trembling when they recalled past valiant deeds.

"So you'll take her in again?" asked Dougal.

"All right," said Simon.

"We'll all do it together," said Madeline,

and Simon (who had been wishing he was twins) was slightly comforted.

Mr Bedwig was the first to see them the next morning: Guinevere, her cage newly cleaned and loaded with provisions, being carefully carried across the playground by Simon and Dougal while Madeline marched solemnly behind.

"Heading for trouble!" exclaimed Mr Bedwig, as he came hurrying up, brandishing an enormous yard brush and clucking with irritation.

"Right then my beauties," he called as soon as he was within calling distance. "Halt! About turn! And double quick march back where you came from!"

"We can't," said Dougal.

"I'll give you can't!" replied Mr Bedwig. "Whatever next? Simon Percy, I would have credited you with more sense!"

"It is for a very good cause," Simon told him earnestly.

"And what might that be?" asked Mr Bedwig sarcastically. "It is Trouble Making and Stirring The Pot and Pushing Your Luck if you ask me. Now hop it before I get cross!"

But even if they had wanted to, it was too

late now to hop it. Mr Jones was bearing down on them at full speed, and moments later Guinevere had been thoroughly and completely confiscated for the second time.

Even Miss Gilhoolie found it difficult to be sorry for Simon that day.

"After all the trouble we had last time," she exclaimed. "I warn you I shall not be offering my diamonds again!"

"There is more to it than meets the eye if you ask me," said Mr Bedwig, who was in and out of Class 4b that morning, busy assembling a slide to go under the trapdoor. "Look at them sitting there as if butter wouldn't melt! They would get no toffee-apples from me. I shall need a volunteer to test this in a minute."

"It is very good of you to take so much trouble," said Miss Gilhoolie.

"No trouble at all," replied Mr Bedwig. "I thought of a fireman's pole, but it wouldn't have done for a lady. Now, Miss Gilhoolie! Choose me a victim and we will see how it goes!"

Miss Gilhoolie said she thought they

should all have a go, and she would guard the door, and this was done, with much smothered laughter and talk of the bad old days when they had been alien life forms in all but habitation. Word had spread through the class that Madeline Brown was going to think of something that would prevent those days ever returning.

"Why me?" wondered Madeline, and then reflected, "I suppose there *is* only me." At the back of her mind was the idea that there *was* something she could do, something she had always known about. It glimmered in her mind like a distant star on a misty night, nearly invisible.

But definitely somewhere, thought Madeline.

Guinevere was released at four o'clock looking rather bemused and Mr Jones made no secret of the fact that she had spent the day under a pile of old curtains.

"She might have suffocated!" squeaked Simon indignantly and Mr Jones said he should have thought of that before. This time he did not lecture Simon as he had the first time, and Simon, who had hoped for a chance to catch sight of the Evidence file, was rather disappointed. Nor, Simon noticed, did Mr Jones once mention Pudding Bags. This pleased him very much.

That night Guinevere began talking the moment Simon switched off the light.

"Bold as brass she offered me a toffee-apple! Bold as brass! You cannot bribe your way out of trouble I told her. I had a letter of complaint about you today. I know, she said, I found it in the bin. How kind of you to spare my feelings!"

Madeline had told Simon that birds learnt better in the dark. It must have been very dark indeed under those curtains, thought Simon, listening in admiration.

"Spare her feelings!" repeated Guinevere furiously. "I would not spare *her*! But there is no Evidence! Evidence, evidence. Silence at all costs!

"Class 4b are being utterly ruined," moaned Guinevere. "Utterly ruined! Lost to me, lost to me and I have no research!"

It was beginning to sound quite sad, thought Simon.

"No research," lamented Guinevere. "No evidence. No appreciation of my methods. Science is the only thing that matters in the end. I should like to see the lot of them blasted into Space!"

He always ends up with Space, thought Simon. He is obsessed.

But Guinevere had not finished yet.

"Toffee-apples, toffee-apples!" she cried. "They stand sucking toffee-apples in MY playground. They are research material, I told her, and you treat them like pets! Horrid little children! If I only had the money I would leave them tomorrow! I should go back to my old life! Back to . . . back to . . ."

Guinevere's voice fell gradually silent.

She's had a long day, thought Simon, and watched lovingly as she tucked her head under her wing, and fell asleep.

"Back to his old life?" asked Madeline Brown when Simon saw her the following Monday. "Are you sure that's what he said?"

"Yes," said Simon. "He's been saying it all weekend. I mean Guinevere has. But afterwards he always says regrets are futile and he still has his great work . . ."

"SILENCE AT ALL COSTS," said Madeline, nodding wisely.

"Yes that one. And he says we are horrid little children only any use for research. And that is all except for stuff about evidence again."

Madeline looked very thoughtful and later she went across the playing field and inspected Mr Bedwig's bonfire site.

Diary of Simon Percy. Thursday, 2nd October

Dougal McDougal has been off sick all this week. I always used to think he was lucky because he only has to sneeze and his mum and his sisters put him to bed with comics and hot lemon and telly in his bedroom and promise him anything he likes.

But poor old Dougal being ill this week of all weeks.

There was a headteacher's conference that Old

Bang Bang had to go to and so he hasn't been in school for three whole days. Our class had a chestnut roast in the basement on the first day and we did a play for Mr Bedwig on the second. It was called The Thirty–Ninth Day and everyone dressed up as animals and we used the fire hoses for rain outside and our classroom was the ark. And Miss Gilhoolie was Noah. Mr Bedwig said it was as good as the real thing and he should know. Today we have had tests all morning which Miss Gilhoolie marked at lunchtime.

You are all far in advance of most children your age, she told us. Which just goes to show what a good teacher I am because you certainly weren't a few weeks ago. I shall reward myself by going to the circus and you can come too. It is supposed to be an excellent one. Real flying horses, they told me at the sweet shop, and no poor tame lions . . .

At the sweetshop? everyone asked.

Where I got the tickets, said Miss Gilhoolie.

I didn't think there would be real flying horses but they were definitely horses and they did fly. We all had goes on them afterwards. Over a safety net in case we fell off. But nobody did.

So poor old Dougal, missing all that.

Simon and Madeline went to visit Dougal that night. They found him sitting up in bed looking the picture of health and very eager to hear the latest news.

"What have you been doing without me?" he demanded at once. "Has anything important happened?"

"No," said Madeline. "Not since we got Guinevere confiscated again and you know about that."

Simon mildly pointed out that there had been the Noah's Ark play (with fire extinguishers), the circus and the chestnut roast, and Madeline said Oh Yes, but those things were not really *very* important.

"Exciting isn't always important," Madeline explained, and Simon said No, he supposed not, and Dougal pounded his bed in fury and demanded to know What Circus? What chestnut roast? What play were they talking about and were they really honestly allowed to use the fire extinguishers for rain?

"Never mind all that now," said Madeline. "There's something I've been thinking about that matters much more. Listen for a minute."

But Dougal did not want to listen for even a second and he turned his unanswered questions upon Simon.

"I'm no good at talking about things," said Simon. "You'd better read my diary."

So Dougal began reading Simon Percy's account of all that he had missed, first to himself, and then aloud. After that, at Madeline's suggestion, he read backwards though the entries until they ended up at the very first morning of term.

There followed a long silence.

"A lot has happened," said Dougal at last. "I'd forgotten half of it. It's a jolly good diary Simon. What's up, Mad?"

Madeline had been staring at Simon as though stunned, but she woke up at Dougal's question and, taking the diary from him, she weighed it in her hands.

"It's much too big," she said eventually. "Even for a class effort. We should be really ill."

"What do you mean?" demanded Simon.

"Perhaps Mr Bedwig could put it in the boiler. I can't think how else we could get rid of it."

"*GET RID OF IT?*"

"Simon," said Madeline calmly. "There is enough evidence in this diary for Mr Jones to get rid of Miss Gilhoolie tomorrow. It doesn't miss a single thing out. Mr Bedwig's slide and the secret tunnel and all the evidence we've eaten and everything we did while he was away. And loads of other things too. All Mr Jones would have to do is show it to the Governors and that would be that. It is highly, highly dangerous. Letters of complaint are *nothing* in comparison."

Then Simon Percy and Madeline Brown had an enormous row.

"I'm not getting rid of it," said Simon, almost crying, because his diary had come to mean more to him than almost anything else in the world and Dougal McDougal backed him up.

Then Madeline flounced off in a huff and Simon, out of gratitude to Dougal, allowed him to borrow his diary for the night so that he could reread the amazing account of all that he had missed. Dougal solemnly promised not to let it out of his sight until Simon collected it the next day.

This did not happen.

The next day two important things happened at once.

The first was that Miss Gilhoolie started them off on a Scientific Art project.

"Space rockets," said Miss Gilhoolie, "and we will stick them all around the walls. They will go nicely with the dragons and cheer up Mr Jones at the same time."

The second important thing was that Dougal McDougal's father returned un-expectedly early from a business trip, discovered Dougal enthroned among his pillows being waited on hand and foot, and sent him immediately back to school.

"You didn't leave my diary behind did you?" demanded Simon the moment he saw him.

" 'Course not." Dougal dumped his over–flowing school bag onto the cloakroom floor with a sigh of relief. "Do you think I'm daft or something? Hang on a minute and I'll find it."

Simon looked doubtfully at Dougal's school bag and thought it would take more than a minute. He was already feeling slightly alarmed, but Dougal, who always enjoyed giving any kind of performance, obviously had no worries at all. He unpacked with the smug cheerfulness of a conjurer producing endless rabbits from an empty hat, and the pile on the cloakroom floor grew and grew.

Dougal's PE kit and one muddy trainer. Two comics with the backs pulled off. A large packed lunch. A burst open packet of crisps.

"Hurry up," said Simon anxiously.

A pencil case with a broken zip. An empty coca cola tin, which judging by the stickiness beneath had not been empty when it was first put in.

"You'd better not have got my diary all gunged up like that," said Simon. "Where is it anyway?"

"Coming, coming," said Dougal airily,

pulling out a broken calculator, a plastic bag full of decomposing conkers and several handfuls of notes and letters to and from school (never delivered).

"It's not there!"

"It is! Somewhere." Dougal dragged out two woolly hats, a Pudding Bag School sweatshirt (Aged 6–8 years), and part of an Action Man.

"That's stuff you've had in your bag for ages!"

"Bother!" said Dougal. "But I did put your diary in! I know I did!" and he turned his school bag upside down and shook a litter of sweet wrappers, odd socks, screwed up tissues and lego onto the cloakroom floor.

"You've lost it," said Simon in horror. "Or left it at home. Might you have left it at home?"

"No. I know I didn't. I put it in and then I remembered my packed lunch . . ."

Mr Bedwig came in at that moment with his arms full of lost property.

"I heard the racket you were making half

way across the playground," he remarked as he came through the door, "Dougal McDougal I have never seen the like! This is a Place of Education not the Council Tip! Get that lot picked up before you say another word! I might have known it was you! You've left a trail clear back to the gates."

They saw then that the Lost Property he was carrying was all Dougal's. His other trainer. His reading books. Two comic covers, a handful of crisps, a broken ruler and a note addressed to Miss Gilhoolie explaining why he had been absent.

"But where is my diary?" wailed Simon, scuffling frantically through the piles of

rubbish on the floor. "Didn't you find my diary Mr Bedwig?"

"I can't say I did," said Mr Bedwig.

Thanks to Mr Bedwig, Class 4b's stock cupboard, that had begun term almost completely empty, was now stuffed with treasure.

"Loot?" said Miss Gilhoolie.

"Well," said Mr Bedwig cryptically, "what I don't happen upon I can usually come by. One way or another. And there's always the sweet shop when absolutely necessary . . ."

Mr Bedwig had a great way of coming by things, and all term he had been visiting Class 4b to remark that he had come by luminous paint, or six pounds of sherbet lemons or gold leaf, or something else of that kind. He would politely ask Miss Gilhoolie if she could be doing with it and she would always politely reply that indeed she could. In the long dreary years before Miss Gilhoolie's arrival Class 4b's artwork had been limited to wax crayon diagrams on the backs of computer printouts, so when she announced the latest new Space Rocket project and threw open the stock cupboard doors there was terrific enthusiasm. People were much too busy to care that Simon Percy had lost his diary and only Dougal McDougal and Madeline Brown understood quite why it mattered so much. Madeline was so cross with Dougal that she could hardly bring herself to speak to him but she managed, despite the awful row of the previous night, to be quite nice to Simon.

"Try not to worry too much," she whispered, pale with worry herself. "He may not have found it and there is still my Idea. I have had it at last and I asked Miss Gilhoolie if she minds if I make a model instead of a picture and she says I can."

Most of Madeline's message meant no sense at all to Simon. Nor had he much hope that Mr Jones had not found his diary, and he could tell from Madeline's face that neither had she. By lunchtime they knew that the worst had happened. A series of enormous notices appeared all over the school.

EXTRAORDINARY AND URGENT GOVERNORS' MEETING TO BE HELD

SUBJECT: SUDDEN ALARMING EVIDENCE FOR IMMEDIATE DISMISSAL OF CERTAIN MEMBER OF STAFF.

"Well, well, well," said Mr Bedwig, seeing Simon studying one of these notices. "And why are you looking so down in the dumps young Simon?"

"He has found my diary," moaned Simon. "The one that me and Dougal were looking for this morning. I lent it to Dougal and he lost it. That is the sudden alarming evidence those notices are about. It is just what Madeline Brown said would happen last night."

"That young lady has more sense than all the rest of you put together if you ask me," remarked Mr Bedwig. "She knows What's What. We have had many a chat and I cannot fault her on her theoretical parachute jumping so I have no doubt she is right about this too. I will see what can be done."

To Simon's immense relief his diary was restored to him before the start of afternoon school.

"I happened upon it," said Mr Bedwig, "while attending the locks on the headmaster's private safe. Now you take it straight home and leave it there Simon. I have had a quick glance and once seen never forgotten as they say. We don't want your Miss Gilhoolie upset and I might not be able to come by it so quick another time."

The notices vanished as rapidly as they had appeared once the sudden and alarming evidence had been restored to its author.

But now, thought Simon, Mr Jones *knew*. And he knew Simon knew he knew. And Simon knew that too. And he wondered if he would ever feel comfortable again.

"I cannot bear it," he told Madeline.

"Perhaps you won't have to much longer," said Madeline. "I shall be able to tell you my idea soon I think. But first, would you mind if I borrowed some of your books? JUNK

MODELLING THAT WORKS, ANYBODY CAN DO ANYTHING, METAL WORK FOR BEGINNERS and that new one you've just got."

"They're very boring," said Simon.

"No they're not," said Madeline. "You'll see."

The day after that Madeline borrowed HOW DOES IT GO? and A CHILD'S GUIDE TO MODERN TECHNOLOGY. In Scientific Art she appeared to do nothing but read, occasionally slipping down Mr Bedwig's slide to consult him in the basement.

"Madeline dear," said Miss Gilhoolie, "are you sure you're not working too hard?"

"Quite sure," said Madeline. "I am only getting on with my model. I will tell you when it's finished Miss Gilhoolie."

"Thank you," said Miss Gilhoolie.

CHAPTER EIGHT

Miss Gilhoolie was looking perplexedly at Madeline's work for Scientific Art. It was a piece of paper about the size of a tablecloth with several smaller sheets attached behind. It looked like a pattern of cobwebs, dozens of cobwebs, layered on top of each other. Hundreds of red pencil arrows led to hundreds of tiny labels. The pages underneath were almost exactly alike, except that the cobweb patterns were different colours and the minute labels were not the same.

"But I thought you were making a model," said Miss Gilhoolie.

"It's a plan of a model," said Madeline.

Miss Gilhoolie peered at some of the tiny labels.

"Mn.Prb.lv." she read. "Mn.Prb.E. Mn.Prb.Fs."

They made no sense at all.

"The top one is the wiring," Madeline told her.

"Well," said Miss Gilhoolie, giving up. "It's very nice Madeline dear, and I can see you have worked very hard . . ."

"Mr Bedwig helped a lot," said Madeline modestly.

". . . But I really don't think we can put it on the wall!"

"Can I take it home then?" asked Madeline, and Miss Gilhoolie said of course she could.

Madeline took her Scientific Art project home and showed it to her father, and he peered at it for several hours and at last announced that he saw no reason at all why it should not work.

"But I trust you won't be leaving us quite yet?" he remarked rather wistfully as he handed it back to Madeline. "I should be very sorry . . . er . . . sorry . . . er . . ."

"Madeline," supplied Madeline, touched by this fatherly affection. "And it is for somebody else, not me."

"Delighted to hear it," said Madeline's father warmly. "Any help you might need, just ask . . . er, Madeline. Always pleased to help with homework, as you know!"

Immensely cheered by this offer, Madeline decided to go public and called a class meeting the very next day. It was held in the middle of the playing field so that there could be no possibility of being overheard.

"This is the problem we have got," began Madeline, plunging straight in. "Mr Jones is planning to get rid of Miss Gilhoolie as soon as possible. He thinks she is spoiling us. She treats us like proper human beings not alien life forms and that is no good for Mr Jones. Also, she isn't frightened of him. He has decided she has got to go and he will be our classteacher again. He wants to use us for his new book which is called SILENCE AT ALL COSTS THE ULTIMATE GUIDE TO THE CONTROL OF ALIEN LIFE FORMS."

There was a murmur of indignation at this revelation. "He cannot just get rid of her without any excuse," went on Madeline, "so he had been collecting evidence . . ."

"But I thought we'd been eating all the evidence," interrupted Samuel. "We have eaten stacks of evidence Madeline, you know we have."

"We have not eaten everything," said Madeline. "We have not eaten Simon's diary for instance. Mr Jones found it earlier this week and if it had not been rescued before the Governors saw it that would have been the end of Miss Gilhoolie. And ever since he saw it he has been worse, hasn't he Simon?"

"Much worse," agreed Simon.

"He will get his evidence one day. I am sure he will. Samantha, crying will not help."

"I can't bear the thought of being an alien life form again," sobbed Samantha. "And I *do* so like Miss Gilhoolie!"

"All of us do," said Madeline kindly. "Anyway, listen, I have thought of a plan to solve all our problems . . ."

Class 4b sighed with relief.

"I think we should build a rocket," said Madeline, as calmly as one might say, "I think we should make a cake". "Mr Jones does not like being a headmaster. He would much rather be an astronaut. If he had a rocket he would be off like a . . ."

"Rocket," finished Dougal McDougal. "But this is completely daft. You don't know how to build a rocket Madeline Brown!"

"Yes I do. I worked out a plan in Scientific Art," said Madeline, holding up her bundle of cobweb diagrams as proof. "Simon lent me some books that explained *exactly* how it should be done, and Mr Bedwig says he will help with the welding, and my father told me that he can see no reason why it should not work . . ."

There was a stunned silence.

"I thought we could build it on Mr Bedwig's bonfire site," Madeline went on. "That way we can cover it up with bits of bonfire when we have to come away. Mr Bedwig has already fixed up some scaffolding made out of odds and ends from the PE cupboard which will be a great help . . . Yes, Samantha?"

"Does Miss Gilhoolie know?"

"Of course not," sighed Madeline. "She would want to know why, and it would hurt her feelings tremendously to hear how much Mr Jones wants to get rid of her. Besides, she would start asking questions about other things. All that evidence we have eaten for a start. She would *not* be pleased about that. Now, this is my idea. When the rocket is finished I shall take Mr Jones to the bonfire site and say, 'Mr Jones, you wanted to go back to your old life and now you can. Here is a rocket . . .' "

"Rockets," interrupted Dougal McDougal, "need rocket engines! Have you thought of that Madeline Brown?"

"Yes I have," said Madeline, "and you can order them from NASA. They deliver within forty-eight hours. The only trouble is they cost quite a lot and you have to be over eighteen. But Mr Jones has all that money he got for his books from Miss Gilhoolie and he is a lot older than eighteen. And when he sees his own private rocket, all finished and provisioned and ready to go except for the engines, he will order them at once and off he will pop and all our troubles will be over. I hope. Any more questions?"

There were no more questions, Madeline's friends being struck dumb with surprise, so Madeline continued. "It will have to be another class effort, this rocket building, and we will have to do it when Mr Jones is not around. That will mean early mornings mostly, and perhaps a bit in the evening between six and seven when he goes to the chip shop for his tea. Somebody will have to be up on the roof watching down Pudding Bag Lane for his car . . ."

"My birthday binoculars!" interrupted Simon excitedly. "We could use my birthday binoculars Madeline!"

"Brilliant," said Madeline. "Thank you Simon! Also we are going to need scrap iron, heat resistant paint, rivets, light bulbs, computer parts and nourishing food, so if anybody . . ."

Simon's sudden enthusiasm was catching. At least a dozen hands shot up with offers of donations.

"And there is keeping it covered up when we're not working on it," said Madeline. "That will take everyone. It is going to get quite big and it is no good Mr Jones seeing it before it is done. He'll just say it's another of Miss Gilhoolie's ideas and get rid of it."

"There's always camouflage!" squeaked Samuel. "I can bring my brother's old army tent."

"It's not going to work," interrupted Dougal suddenly. "All this is just rubbish! Even if you could fix them together you'd never get enough rocket parts in the first place. And anyway it would take years!"

"Not with all of us helping, and Mr Bedwig too," argued Madeline. "You know what a fast worker he is! And he has promised to see what he can come by in the way of bits and pieces and he says there is always the sweet shop if absolutely necessary . . ."

The mention of the sweet shop convinced even the most doubtful. Madeline suddenly felt very tired. "That is the end of the meeting," she said thankfully, and sat down to thunderous applause.

From that moment on the secret rocket

project became a phenomenal success. Sheet metal, pot rivets, star maps and provisions were donated in unlimited quantities, begged by Class 4b from their friends and relations, who said that it made a nice change from the Jam and Good Quality Jumble they were usually expected to provide.

For security reasons no grown-ups were allowed into the secret, except for Mr Bedwig (who of course had been in on it right from the beginning), Madeline's father (who now spent many hours checking computer programs in the belief that he was helping with homework), and Simon's Gran, whose kitchen window happened to overlook the launch pad.

"I am sure they will both be quite safe," said Madeline. "My father will be anyway. Ordinary people never listen to a word he says. Only bonkers professors take any notice of him. And nobody takes any notice of *them*."

"People don't really listen to Gran either," agreed Simon. "They just say she is wonderful for her age. Let's invite her to come and look properly! After all, she did buy all the instruction books."

"Let's invite them both," proposed Madeline, and this was done straight away.

"Class 4b, you are up to something!" said Miss Gilhoolie one morning.

Class 4b, their hands black from early morning rocket engineering and their eyes gleaming with secrets, grinned and made no comment.

"And where is Simon Percy?"

A strange scraping sound from overhead answered that question. Class 4b rushed outside and were just in time to see Simon as he slithered, fast asleep, down the sloping roof, hung for a moment from the guttering, and then tumbled (still sleeping) into the arms of his fellow classmates. They carried him inside and dumped him on his seat where he woke up at once, said, "Sorry I'm late Miss Gilhoolie," and began polishing his binoculars.

"Is everything all right, Simon?" asked Miss Gilhoolie.

"Yes thank you," said Simon politely.

The enthusiasm of Class 4b, the tremendous efficiency of Mr Bedwig, and the quite astonishing way in which Pudding Bag Lane sweet shop supplied endless vital rocket components (while remaining firmly closed to all passing trade) combined to work wonders. The rocket was very nearly complete when Simon's Gran and Madeline's father paid their visit. It was an impressive sight. It rose above Mr Bedwig's scaffolding into a five metre high shining tower. At the top a fluted dustbin lid had been transformed into an elegant cone. The port holes (old washing machine doors) were newly polished. The emergency exit (ex–Pudding Bag Lane Canning Factory and in previous life a giant sized pressure cooker lid) was outlined in gleaming red paint, and the entrance door (ex–Disneyland, Paris, happened upon one holiday by Mr Bedwig) was edged in holly green. The whole of the rest of the rocket, including the four large dustbins at its base which would one day hold the engines, had been sprayed with

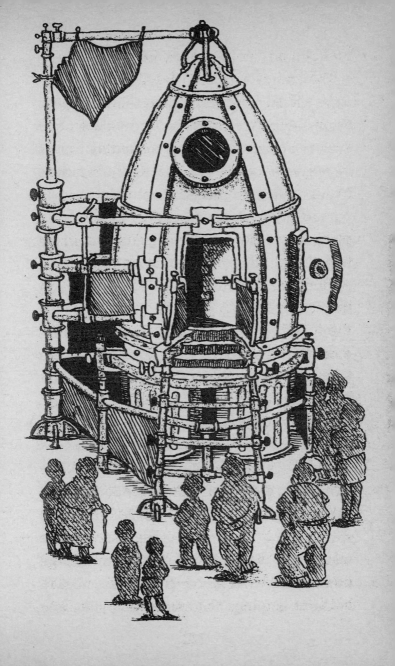

Non-Stick-Heat-Resistant-Radiation-Proof-Easy-Clean-Anti-Mildew-Guaranteed-Rust-Retarding-Glitter-Effect-Silver paint. (Supplied on credit by the sweet shop.)

"It is a remarkable achievement for a class of ten year olds," said Madeline's father. "Very promising indeed!"

"Yes indeed," agreed Gran, as she peered carefully into the crowd that surrounded the rocket. "Ah, there is dear Madeline! I must go and give her this tin. It is a Keeping Fruit Cake to set him on his way. And I also have some packets of seeds. Peas, carrots, onions, parsley and potato," she explained, seeing Professor Brown's look of bewilderment. "Just the basis of a good Vegetable Soup . . ." and she hobbled away to where Madeline stood in the centre of an admiring crowd.

"Madeline Brown is getting jolly big–headed these days," Dougal McDougal said resentfully to himself, as he watched the scene from the look–out post on the school roof. "It's only a perfectly ordinary rocket! Without engines. It looks exactly like any other rocket. Probably smaller actually. And it wobbles!"

"It wobbles!" he told Madeline later on when he was back on solid ground again.

"It just needs ballast. I'm going to use Mr Jones' PRACTICAL PUNISHMENT books. I'll ask to borrow them. Miss Gilhoolie won't mind."

"I suppose you think you're jolly clever," said Dougal, who was tired and cold and not at all pleased that his wobble was being disposed of so efficiently. "But you're not! You'd never have managed without Mr Bedwig, and everyone helping all the time, and the stuff you've had from the sweet shop! All this fuss is just showing off!"

This was most unfair, because Madeline never showed off about anything.

"You're just jealous," she replied crossly because she was rather hurt. "Jealous, because I thought of it and you never could!"

This was true but tactless and it brought out the worst in Dougal. He answered that she thought she was the only person in the world who could think of things. And that she was wrong. And that he would show her.

"How?" demanded Madeline.

"Wait and see," said Dougal.

Dougal and Madeline are quarrelling again, wrote Simon in his diary that night. *They have not been friends since Dougal stuck up for me about not getting rid of my diary and then lost it the next day. I wish he hadn't. Old Bang Bang is in and out of our classroom all the time now and he is always glaring at me. He is looking for my diary I know. He did not like our Scientific Art at all. He made Miss Gilhoolie take it down again.*

Drat that miserable man! said Miss Gilhoolie.

She has lent Madeline Brown all her boxes of the PRACTICAL PUNISHMENT books.

Would you be cross if they got a bit changed? asked Madeline.

Anything would be an improvement, said Miss Gilhoolie. What sort of changed?

Hot, said Madeline.

You can roast them for all I care, said Miss Gilhoolie. They are Utter Bunk. Good grief! Here is Mr Jones AGAIN! What can we do for you THIS TIME Mr Jones.

I am just checking the items on your Interest Table, said Mr Jones. No parrots, I trust.

Certainly not, said Miss Gilhoolie. The children keep their treasures safely at home these days. Anyway, I imagine dear Guinevere has better things to do with her time.

Keep them at home, do they? said Mr Jones.

He stayed away after that.

After that last entry, life in Pudding Bag School was never quite the same again.

CHAPTER NINE

Simon closed his diary, pushed it under his pillow and switched off his bedside light. This was Guinevere's signal and she began at once. She had never forgotten the time she had spent as a prisoner of Mr Bang Bang Jones, and she seemed determined that Simon should never forget it too. Her nightly recital was becoming as familiar to him as the chimings of the church clock across the road.

". . . Original Pudding Bag! . . . I have brought sandwiches, sandwiches, thank you Miss! . . . Evidence, evidence. Evidence for the dismissal of Guinevere Gilhoolie . . ."

Simon reached under his pillow just to make quite sure that his diary was still there. Even after so many nights of falling asleep to Guinevere's reminiscences he still found the process rather unnerving.

". . . Hard work and Science! . . . Research material and she treats them like pets . . . Silence at all costs! . . ."

"Oh shut up Guinevere!" moaned Simon, but very quietly because he knew she could not help it.

". . . Bangs and blue flashes! That idiotic caretaker has wired it to the mains!"

(Simon always rather liked that bit, that and the toffee-apples, which happened to come next that night.)

". . . Offered me a toffee-apple, bold as brass! . . . How I wish I could go back to my old life!"

"Perhaps you will do soon," said Simon drowsily.

"One more day's work," Madeline had announced that afternoon. "There's just a little bit of painting to finish. I will do it tomorrow, and on Wednesday I will take Mr Jones to see his rocket. The engines will take no time to fit, it is just a matter of slotting them into the dustbins. If he orders them straight away and it really is forty-eight hours for delivery . . . Forty-eight hours . . . That is two days . . . He could be off by Friday," Madeline calculated.

"Friday," Dougal McDougal had repeated scornfully. "And today's only Monday! That's no good! That means he's still got a whole week to collect his evidence. Fat lot of good it will be launching Old Bang Bang into space if he's managed to get rid of Miss Gilhoolie before he goes! You want to get rid of him a lot sooner than Friday Madeline Brown."

"I want to," Madeline had agreed. "But I can't. No one could. And don't say you could because you couldn't!"

"Oh couldn't I then?" Dougal had replied immediately, simply for the sake of having the last word, and then he had said more thoughtfully, "Couldn't I?"

Mr Bedwig brought a large parcel to Madeline that afternoon.

"What is it?" Dougal had asked inquisitively.

"Never you mind," said Mr Bedwig. "It is not something as wants packing and

130

unpacking more than is strictly necessary. It is an Emergency Precaution in case of the Unexpected. I happened on it quite by chance and I thought of Young Madeline at once! And you keep it with you, Madeline. Better safe than sorry when it comes to rockets!"

"Thank you very much," said Madeline, seeming to guess almost at once what was in Mr Bedwig's parcel.

"I hope you don't need it," stressed Mr Bedwig.

"I hope I don't too," agreed Madeline.

"I wonder what it was," murmured Simon, nearly asleep. "I wish it was Friday now and Mr Jones was safely out of the way."

"Evidence," muttered Guinevere, with her head beneath her wing. "Evi . . . evi . . . evi . . ." and she gave a tired chirrup, and was silent.

It took Dougal McDougal a long time to solve the problem of how to show Madeline Brown that she was not the only person in the world

who could think of things. It was very difficult because Madeline had thought of a rocket. Which meant that Dougal had to think of something more spectacular than a rocket. Dougal had left the school playing field and was wandering down Pudding Bag Lane racking his brains but no good ideas seemed to come. At the sweet shop he stopped to re-read the poster and to try the door handle. Lately it had begun to look quite shiny from the persistent efforts of Class 4b to come in and buy something absolutely necessary, although exactly what they could never decide.

So far, however, the sweet shop had remained stubbornly closed. Nor did it open for Dougal, but just as he touched the handle inspiration came to him. Madeline's rocket had one great flaw. It had no engines. It could not be launched into space without the co-operation of NASA and Mr Bang Bang Jones.

"Or me!" said Dougal McDougal exultantly, because now he had a plan. A joke. A huge surprise for Class 4b and Madeline Brown in particular. Something that would make Madeline exclaim: "I wish I'd had that brilliant idea! I wish I'd thought of doing it like that!"

When Madeline said that, Dougal decided, everything would change. Straight away he would tell her how good her rocket was, and he would apologise to Simon for losing his diary. He would become once again his usual modest, charming, and wonderful self.

"But Madeline has to say it first," said Dougal.

It was black dark. It was the middle of the night and there was no moon.

"Evidence! Evidence! Evidence!"

Bother Guinevere! thought Simon, fast asleep.

"Silence at all costs!"

Simon groaned and slid down in bed so that the quilt covered his ears.

"Dratted parrot!"

Simon, still dreaming, burrowed completely under the bedclothes.

"Evidence! Evidence! Evidence!" shrieked Guinevere, every feather quivering.

The dark figure that stooped over the bed turned around and glared in irritation.

". . . Original Pudding Bag!"

Long white fingers groped hastily around the floor, over the bedside table, under the pillow. Grabbed.

The grab woke Simon at last. He sat up

and a gust of freezing air hit him in the face. A clattering sound came from the street below. The bedroom window was wide open and the curtains were streaming into the room on the cold night wind. Guinevere was frantic. His diary was gone.

Dougal lay awake that night thinking of ways and means, and the next morning he set to work.

The first thing he needed was a day off school to arrange everything. This was no problem at all. His mother and father departed early for work leaving his seven adoring sisters in charge. It only took a little sighing, a groan or two, and a small display of struggling with the enormous breakfast they had cooked for him to make all seven of them look at each other and decide poor darling Dougal had been working too hard.

"Take a day off, Dougal!" they urged as they whirled around the house in a chaos of hairdryers, lipsticks and slimming magazines, preparing for work, so Dougal did.

The next thing he needed was money. Quite a lot of money. This was also easy. He borrowed it from his sisters as they dashed past, late as usual for their buses and tubes and offices and appointments.

"Take what you like Dougal Darling!" they said, handing over notes and cash and handfuls of credit cards while he straddled the doorway like a miniature highway man. "Take what you like BUT GET OUT OF THE WAY!"

By lunchtime only Dougal and his youngest elder sister, Kate, were left in the house. Kate did not go to work. She was supposed to go to college, but she very seldom did. She preferred to stay at home, confident that one day something would turn up to prevent her ever having to earn a living. Kate was extremely pretty and extremely good natured and easily Dougal's favourite sister. Also, she was over eighteen (which mattered very much), fond of shopping, and had passed her driving test. She made no difficulty at all about driving Dougal in the family minibus to Pudding Bag Lane.

"But you'll have to stay outside and look after it, Dougal," she told him.

"Why?" asked Dougal, outraged.

"Because last time I borrowed it, it got stolen," said Kate. "And two times before it got driven into. And every other time I've locked the keys inside by accident. So say you will Dougal darling, or else I'm not taking you anywhere!"

"All right, I will," agreed Dougal, but he thought that the hardest part of his whole plan would be waiting outside in the minibus while his sister Kate turned the handle of the Pudding Bag Lane sweet shop and went inside.

While Dougal and Kate were shopping, Pudding Bag School was in a state of turmoil. The story of Simon's burglary spread like wildfire and any faint doubts as to who the burglar might be were dispelled as soon as the notices appeared.

EXTRAORDINARY AND URGENT GOVERNORS' MEETING TO BE HELD TODAY!

OBJECT: INSTANT DISMISSAL OF DANGEROUS AND INCAPABLE MEMBER OF STAFF

"It is very sad," said Miss Gilhoolie to

Samantha when she found her crying over one of these communications. "But Mr Jones is quite right. Dangerous and incapable members of staff should be dismissed."

"But Miss Gilhoolie," sobbed Samantha. "Don't you know who he means?"

"No," said Miss Gilhoolie, adding firmly, "and idle speculation would not be kind! Now, books away! Bad news I'm afraid! Spelling Test time! All the words you have learnt this term!"

This was a very dismal prospect because all term Miss Gilhoolie had dished out ten words a night, five nights a week, with triple helpings on Fridays, no excuses accepted, and it made a very long list. They were about half-way through when the door crashed open.

"Number one hundred and twenty-nine," said Miss Gilhoolie. "Mephistopheles. Good morning Mr Jones!"

Mr Jones did not reply. Instead he stood and shrieked with laughter. He howled. He rocked with glee, doubled up. He pointed a trembling finger at Miss Gilhoolie and hugged his chest and screeched.

It was a horrible performance.

"He is choking," declared Miss Gilhoolie suddenly. "Mr Jones, I will pat your back. Madeline dear, please fetch Mr Jones a glass of water . . ."

But Mr Jones had gone as suddenly as he had appeared.

"Oh," said Miss Gilhoolie as the door slammed behind him. "Well. Sit down then Madeline and we will continue. Number one hundred and thirty. Philosophy. What has anyone noticed about the last ten words?"

"They are PH words Miss Gilhoolie," said Madeline Brown.

"Quite right Madeline," said Miss Gilhoolie. "Now, on to the dinosaurs! Number one hundred and forty-one: Diplodocus!"

At lunchtime Simon and Madeline, remembering how Mr Bedwig recovered the diary when it went missing the first time, paid an urgent visit to the basement.

"Cheer up Simon," said Madeline hopefully. "He got it back straight away before."

But for once Mr Bedwig was no help at all. The boiler was out of sorts and the basement was miserable with smoke and Mr Bedwig was in a depressed and fatalistic mood.

"If you've come to me about them notices you can forget it," he told them grumpily, "I have problems enough of my own. It is obsolete that boiler, they would have chucked it out of the ark. I shall get proper solar panels rigged up when I get five minutes' peace. Which I never shall. And I thought I told you to keep that diary out of school Sir Lancelot."

"I was burgled," said Simon.

"Well, it is beyond me this time. I had a look round his office first thing but it was not there. It is my belief he has it on his person. There is no help for it to my way of thinking. What's to be will be and nature will take its course."

"Oh Mr Bedwig!" wailed Simon and Madeline.

"Don't you come Oh Mr Bedwigging me!" said Mr Bedwig, poking gloomily through a box of broken table–tennis bats. "Look at this lot! There are not two the same size! What can't be cured must be endured. Now go and put that last drop of paint on yon rocket before the bell goes."

"What's the point anymore?" asked Madeline. "Mr Jones will have got rid of poor Miss Gilhoolie long before it's ready to launch. Dougal McDougal was quite right. Everyone is saying so now."

"Be that as it may," said Mr Bedwig. "You must prepare for all eventualities. Noah built that ark through a record breaking drought. Still got that Emergency Precaution with you?"

Madeline nodded and indicated the school bag strapped across her shoulders.

"Off with you then," said Mr Bedwig, and handed her the paint.

"I shouldn't mind working there!" said Kate, hopping into the driver's seat, starting the engine, and pulling out without looking in front of a double decker bus.

"Oy!" cried Dougal. "Watch out Kate! And why are we going? Aren't we going to load them up? Didn't you buy any?"

"Ever such a nice lad," said Kate. "They're being delivered."

"Delivered?"

"Mmmmm."

"What do you mean, delivered? Kate! Those lights are red!"

Kate did a perfect controlled emergency stop, took out a hairbrush and began to tidy her long blonde hair.

"*Don't* grow up to be a back seat driver Dougal darling," she said plaintively.

"But what do you mean, being delivered?"

"It means they bring them for you," said Kate patiently, grovelling under her seat, retrieving a dropped lipstick, and beginning to apply it very carefully. "Bother these lights! They never give you time to do anything."

"Everyone's beeping us," said Dougal in anguish. "*Please* get on and tell me what happened."

"Hang on a minute." Kate leaned out of her window, waved cheerfully at the frantic line of drivers behind her, and yelled, "Sorry! Lips!" pointing to her lips.

"Red again now anyway," she said, coming back in. "You watch. They'll change any second. See!"

"Go then!" groaned Dougal. "Why don't you go?"

"I was *showing* you," explained Kate, above the cacophony of horns behind her. "I'll go next time. There."

"*Please* tell me what happened in the sweet shop," begged Dougal as she swerved into a bus lane and began humming happily to herself.

"Well. He said, 'What about the zoo, Saturday?' and I said, 'Oh I love the animals but the cages make me cry,' and he said 'I'm making a list of what needs doing. You could always help . . .' "

"WHO DID?"

"Peter from the sweet shop. All these roundabouts! How many times have I been round this one?"

"I don't know."

"Well I'm getting fed up of it! Hang on!"

Dougal clenched his teeth and shut his eyes.

"There we are," said Kate. "Only I think I'm lost. Never mind, we can just keep going. Yes well, I went in and there was Peter and I said 'Do you sell fireworks please?' and Peter said 'Certainly darl ... Madam, any particular sort?' So I said 'Rockets'. That's what you wanted isn't it?"

Dougal nodded.

" 'Rockets,' he said. 'How many are you thinking of?' OH DOUGAL! THE POOR LITTLE SQUIRREL! OH, THE POOR LITTLE SQUIRREL! Oh, it's all right. I'm going to stop somewhere. Through that gap."

"It's St James's Park."

"I know. Isn't it lovely? And that means we're not lost. 'Four dustbins full my brother wants,' I told Peter. 'For his school project. He goes to Pudding Bag School, poor little soul!' 'Oh right,' said Peter. 'Ready to go then are they? We thought they were doing it through NASA ...' What did he mean?"

"Nothing. Go on."

"Well I didn't have any choice because Peter said there was only one brand would

145

do it. The InterGalactic Special Effect Solar somethings. 'Sounds lovely,' I said, and he said, 'Delivered and packed?' So I said, 'Packed and delivered you mean!' and he said, 'No, delivered and packed. We can put them in the bins for you if you'd like,' and I said that sounds much safer than my little brother doing it, and he said, 'Right Oh! I'll get on to it straight away!' and he wouldn't let me pay. He said 'Just sign here and I'll put it on the account.' So I did."

Brilliant, wonderful Kate! thought Dougal,

proudly, letting out a huge sigh of relief.

"Then what?" he demanded.

"Well I signed and he read it and he said, 'Kate is a lovely name! Kate just suits you.' And we talked about the zoo. Look Dougal! Four policemen all together! You hardly ever see four policemen all together! I hope there's nothing wrong with the ducks . . ."

Then Kate was arrested.

"Tell Peter!" she screeched over her shoulder as they led her away.

Somehow or another the afternoon at Pudding Bag School dragged past. Four o'clock arrived and Class 4b were dismissed with their usual spelling list and the awful feeling that once the Extraordinary and Urgent Governors' meeting had taken place there would be nobody to care whether they knew the words or not.

"We will always love you Miss Gilhoolie," sobbed Samantha as they lined up to go home.

"I should hope so too," said Miss Gilhoolie.

Madeline and Simon found themselves unable to leave. They hung about the outbuildings, waiting for the moment when the Governors would assemble and the final act would begin.

The lollipop lady departed and the cleaners arrived. Lights and vacuum cleaners were switched on. Dusk fell over the playground, and one by one the lights went off again. The cleaners left in a gossiping huddle and the school stood dark and silent except for the main entrance and Mr Jones' office. Madeline and Simon could see him in there, arranging chairs for the fatal meeting. Occasionally he stopped work to double up in silent laughter.

"There's your diary!" said Madeline suddenly, and there it was, battered and unmistakable, on Mr Jones' desk.

"I wonder where he's had it all day."

"He's taking it with him now."

Mr Jones vanished then, but reappeared a few minutes later, silhouetted in the open doorway of the main entrance, rocking on his heels. In his fists he clutched Simon's diary. The Governors were due any minute and victory was within his grasp at last. His glee was awful to behold, but it didn't last long.

The sight of his stolen diary in the hands of its thief was too much for Simon Percy. Hurtling out of the shadows, he charged across to Mr Jones, seized his diary and fled. He dashed across the playground and in a black corner of the bike sheds paused, and tried to think.

The trouble was that there was no place to run and no place to hide. Home was impossible, there were Gran and Guinevere to be considered. Also Mr Jones knew where it was and would certainly find him. Pudding Bag Lane was dark and uninviting. The playground was an empty waste.

There was a flurry of motion and Madeline was beside him. "Quick Simon, he's just coming now!" she had time to pant, and then Mr Jones arrived thundering round the corner and the chase began.

It was like some awful game of tag. Simon ran and ran, scurrying backwards and forwards across the playground, pounding round corners, sprinting across the places where the light streamed out from windows, hugging his diary, dodging and leaping and always with Mr Jones one breath behind.

"Drop it! Drop it!" roared Mr Jones.

A stitch began in Simon's side and he was finding it hard to breathe. He could hear Madeline shouting at him, but his brain made no sense of the words. It became like a dream and he ran in his sleep. He stopped being frightened and then became terribly frightened, and then tripped.

"Ha!" panted Mr Jones in victory, and the next moment the diary was plucked from Simon's hands, but not by Mr Jones.

Just in time Madeline had seized it, and she ran with it straight to the place that had filled her thoughts for days. Straight to the bonfire site and Mr Jones' rocket, and Mr Jones ran straight after her.

It took Dougal a very long time to get from St James's Park to the Pudding Bag Lane sweet shop. It was nearly dark when he arrived. He hurled himself at the door and it opened before he touched it so that he landed on the chest of a large young man.

"Just closing," said the young man, removing Dougal and depositing him in the street before turning to lock the door behind him. "Not absolutely necessary, is it?"

"Kate said, 'Tell Peter!' " gasped Dougal. "My sister Kate! She's been arrested!"

"Kate who bought the rockets?"

"Yes, yes! In St James's Park!"

"I'll get there at once."

"Are you Peter then? Did you deliver them?"

"Come on out of the way!"

"I only wondered . . ." began Dougal, but it was no good. Peter was already sprinting down Pudding Bag Lane, his hair on end and his jacket flying open as he charged to the rescue. As he turned the corner something fell out of his pocket. Dougal followed him and picked it up. It was a box of matches.

By the time Dougal had straightened up Peter had vanished. Dougal stood alone in the darkening lane and for the first time it dawned on him that he had done it. He had thought of a way of getting Old Bang Bang Jones into space before Friday. No need now to wait for engines from NASA, the rocket was complete and ready to go. He had beaten Madeline Brown.

I'll just go and have a look, thought Dougal.

Madeline reached the rocket with no clear plan in mind except perhaps to lock herself in with Simon's diary and stay there, if necessary, until morning. That would prevent the Governors' meeting going ahead at least, and during the night she might think of something better. It seemed to be the best she could do.

She reached the rocket, and then things began to go wrong. The door was stiffer than she had anticipated. The darkness was confusing and she was out of breath, and Mr Jones' footsteps had been muffled on the grass. He was much nearer than she knew. Before she could close the door he had caught up with her.

Dougal McDougal heard nothing of the

chase. He came up to the bonfire site just in time to see Mr Jones clamber aboard before the door slammed shut.

Then Dougal had a stupendous and terrible idea.

There was Mr Jones' rocket, finished at last. There was Mr Jones inside it. The bonfire was ready and the engines were primed. There was a box of matches in Dougal's pocket.

The temptation was too great. Dougal sprinted across the shadowy, trodden grass, pulled out the matches, and lit the bonfire.

CHAPTER TEN

The flames took hold almost at once and Dougal, remembering that the rockets he had had delivered and packed were of the InterGalactic Special Effect Solar something variety, prudently retreated to the middle of the playing field to watch from a safe distance. There he was astonished to find Simon Percy, wheezing terribly, and staggering towards him.

"Dougal! Dougal! Quick!" croaked Simon flapping his arms in a kind of slow motion of despair. "Quick Dougal! We've got to call the fire brigade! Someone's lit the bonfire!"

"I know," said Dougal smugly. "It was me."

Simon goggled at him.

"It's a surprise for Madeline."

Simon could make no sense of this.

"The fire brigade," he repeated frantically.

"You go. I can't run anymore."

"Don't be daft," said Dougal. "You don't want to miss the best bit do you? It's going to take off any minute."

"Take off?"

"Those dustbin engines are stuffed full of firework rockets! InterGalactic Special Effect Solar somethings . . ."

Even as he spoke there came from the bonfire site a most enormous fizzing pop.

The ground rocked beneath their feet. The entire end of the playing field became a glowing cloud of greenish purple smoke. A terrible hissing roar began to fill the whole night. It grew louder and louder and constellations of stars began hurtling to the ground. Simon's legs gave way completely. He collapsed onto the grass and shut his eyes and hoped he was witnessing the end of the world.

Beside him Dougal said, "There she goes!"

Simon's eyes opened to an unbelievable sight. Madeline's rocket rising straight up to the sky in a cloud of stars. Rainbow and silver coloured stars that leapt in curves from

the dustbin engines and vanished with pops and whistles and coloured smoke.

"Guess who's on board?" said Dougal complacently.

"Madeline," moaned Simon.

"No! Twit! Old Bang Bang Jones!"

"And Madeline."

"Don't be daft."

"She is. I saw her. She was saving my diary. Mr Jones was after her . . ."

"Mr Jones is on the rocket! I saw him! He climbed on board and the door banged shut . . ."

"After Madeline."

"NO!"

"YES! HE CLIMBED IN AFTER MADELINE."

"HE DIDN'T."

"HE DID. HE CLIMBED IN AFTER MADELINE. MADELINE'S IN THE ROCKET."

"I WON'T LISTEN. I'M NOT LISTENING."

"SHE IS. SHE'S UP THERE NOW."

"Say you're joking," begged Dougal.

"I'm not joking. Look at me. I'm not joking."

Dougal looked and saw that he wasn't. They stared at each other and then they stared up into the sky.

There was nearly nothing to be seen. A small blur of light. A smudge of cloud that seemed to sparkle. That was all.

Inside the rocket it was very bumpy. Bumpy and dark, pitch black, with blinding white flashes.

At first Madeline and Old Bang Bang were too startled to do anything but hold on, but after a while the motion became smoother, Madeline found the light switch, and they were able to dodge the quite astonishing amount of loose objects that were tumbling about them.

But neither of them said a word. Old Bang Bang's mouth was hanging open and his eyes were bulging out of his head but he did not make a single sound. Madeline thought it was like being at a terrible party where no one can bring themselves to break the quiet.

She waited and waited and when at last she could bear it no longer she said, "I can't think *why* it took off."

Old Bang Bang's voice seemed to come from far, far away. He said, "What took off?"

"This. This rocket we made for you."

"Rocket."

"Yes. For you. Because you said you wanted to go back to your old life."

"You made this?"

"Yes."

There was an even longer silence, broken only by the sound of external explosions. Madeline began to feel terribly awkward.

"It's very small," said Old Bang Bang.

"It will look better tidied up," said Madeline. "It's only meant for one person really."

"One person? *One* person?"

"Yes," admitted Madeline, as she stacked and tidied. "Well, we thought, just you really, you know . . ."

"You are telling me that this rocket was designed to carry one person alone?" interrupted Mr Jones.

"Yes. I really shouldn't be here."

"No you *shouldn't*," shouted Old Bang Bang Jones, suddenly leaping into action. "You certainly shouldn't! Think of the weight. You are extra weight!"

"Perhaps we should throw out the ballast."

"The ballast?"

"PRACTICAL PUNISHMENTS. We won't need them, will we? We could thr—"

"*Throw out* PRACTICAL PUNISHMENTS," roared Old Bang Bang, "*With new worlds to conquer! You silly, silly child! Out you get!*"

"What?"

"Out! Out!" repeated Old Bang Bang. "What are you waiting for? I must be on my way!"

"But Mr Jones . . ."

"I hope I have made myself perfectly clear?"

"Yes, yes," said Madeline, "but, Mr Jones, you don't know how to fly it . . ."

"Mere common sense!"

"Or where things are. There are star maps, and a first aid box and Simon Percy's gran's fruit cake which she said ought to be kept wrapped up for another two weeks . . ."

"I cannot listen to all this chatter! Out you go! You are wasting my time!"

"I will, I will," said Madeline, desperately. "It will be quite all right. I have an Emergency Precaution. You need not worry . . ."

"I am not worrying," said Old Bang Bang coldly as he fumbled with the lock on the Emergency Exit. "Ah! There! Got it! Off you go!"

He would have thrown me out anyway! thought Madeline suddenly. Emergency Precaution or not! Dear Mr Bedwig. Oh, *Dear* Mr Bedwig! And I always knew Theoretical Parachute Jumping would come in handy.

A blast of cold air suddenly filled the rocket.

"Now then," said Old Bang Bang, hustling her toward the icy black hole. "Out with you! Before I get cross!"

"Yes," said Madeline bravely, "But Mr Jones . . ."

"What is it now? I need to shut the door!"

"Only, there are sandwiches under the black box that need eating straight away. And a hot water bottle . . ."

Mr Jones gave a hard push and Madeline suddenly found herself swinging by her finger tips from the edge of the hole.

"Let go at once!" snapped Mr Jones.

"Are you *quite* sure you wouldn't like to come too?"

"Let go at once!" shouted Mr Jones, so Madeline let go.

Madeline never forgot the few minutes that followed, free falling through the solar system, fumbling with frozen fingers to undo the straps of her school bag.

"I know I *should* have enjoyed it," she told people afterwards.

"Didn't you then?"

"Only in a way."

Simon and Dougal also never forgot those minutes. Quite a crowd had gathered at the bonfire site. Miss Gilhoolie and Mr Bedwig, who had been stripping down the boiler in the basement, and who had rushed out at the sound of the first explosion. Guinevere and Gran, and Madeline's father who had been visiting them for tea. Several strangers from the sweet shop and all the School Governors. The story of Dougal's rash and highly dangerous action had spread very quickly and nobody was being very friendly towards him. He had a horrible feeling that he would be dealt with later. Mr Bedwig had already hinted something of the kind, but right now all anyone could concentrate on was the patch of night sky where the rocket had last been visible.

A tiny speck of movement appeared in the blackness. It travelled so fast that it was only a blur of motion.

"It's a bit of rocket," said Simon.

"It's Madeline," said Miss Gilhoolie, and there was absolute silence.

She fell like a star, plummeting, and then, at the moment when the crowd on the ground could bear to look no longer, something changed, and she fell like an Autumn leaf.

"Good girl," said Mr Bedwig approvingly. "She's found the rip cord!"

An enormous parachute, gold as an Autumn beech tree, now billowed above Madeline.

"I came by that," said Mr Bedwig, wiping a tear from his eye, "not a week ago. I gave it to her just in case."

"I think she's still got my diary," whispered Simon.

"She's waving," said Dougal, "and listen! What is she shouting?"

"I can't *think* why it took off!" shouted Madeline.

CHAPTER ELEVEN

Dougal, Madeline and Simon met outside the sweet shop before school the following morning. The door was wide open.

"Bootlaces, flying saucers, bubble gum or chews?" demanded an old woman from behind the counter. "That's all we've got. I have been in hospital and that lot that took over never kept up the stock!"

Tentatively they glanced at each other, and then one after another, stepped inside.

"Hopped it they have!" continued the old woman crossly. "Without a word or a sign! Unless you'd count that!" And she pointed to a bit of card propped up against the counter.

SIMPLY THE BEST!
Due to the early completion of work in this area we have moved to a new location.

"They've gone then," said Simon, and stood and wondered and wondered, while Dougal and Madeline bought ancient twopenny chews, bubble gum in faded wrappers, melting red bootlaces and damp flying saucers.

"There's something very odd about that sweet shop," said Dougal as they walked slowly on to school.

"Not any more," said Madeline sadly.

From the diary of Simon Percy,
Pudding Bag School,
Pudding Bag Lane,
London,
England,
Great Britain,
The World,
Space.

Monday, 20th October

Miss Gilhoolie came to school today in silver leather jeans and all her diamonds.

What do you think Simon? she said and I said, Oh Miss LeatherGilhoolie, Oh Miss Leather-Gilhoolie you do look lovely and shiney.

That's right Simon, she said. It may not be National Curriculum but it is very important to remember that anything goes with diamonds.

Dougal McDougal is being very kind to everyone. When Madeline heard about why her rocket took off she said, Oh Dougal! I wish I'd had that brilliant idea! I wish I'd thought of doing it like that!

Madeline is feeling a bit guilty because she

167

didn't bring Old Bang Bang with her when she
parachuted down. She did ask him, but she didn't
like to try and persuade him, she said, in case the
parachute didn't open. Because up until then she
had only done theoretical parachute jumping and
she wasn't sure it would. But Miss Gilhoolie says,
Do not worry Madeline. I am sure he is much
happier where he is.

Kate did not go to prison. You cannot go to
prison just for parking on grass, even if it is the
grass of St James's Park. Dougal says he thinks
she forgot all about going with Peter to the zoo
last Saturday. He says she just hums very loudly
every time he tries to ask her.

Now that Mr Jones has gone Mr Bedwig is
Acting Head but he is still caretaker too.

It has happened before, he says, even Old Noah
wasn't above getting down with a bucket when
the need arose. But that was a Short Term
Arrangement due to an Emergency.

So is this, said Miss Gilhoolie, and I expect you
will get double pay while you do it.

Money, said Mr Bedwig. I do this job for love
not money.

I bring in Guinevere every day now, to keep

168

Mr Bedwig company when he is having to be Headmaster. She has learned to say a lot of things that are much nicer to listen to in the night, and she has learnt to whistle a song that Mr Bedwig sings to her.

Oh Guinevere, Sweet Guinevere,
The years may come, and the years may go,
But still my heart holds memories dear
The dreams and songs of long ago.

And I think it's lovely.

And so everything is all right. Nearly all right. But I never got my birthday wish and now that the sweet shop is just a sweet shop again I don't suppose I ever shall. I am exactly ten years and six weeks old now.

I wished it had been years, not days. Then they would have been back quite soon.

That was my birthday wish. Never tell, Gran said, but writing is not the same as telling.

I wish it had been years, not days.

For a few moments Simon stared at the words he had written and in his mind he was back once more in the end of summer park on the last day of the holidays. He saw again the short dry grass of the birthday picnic, the hot shimmer of the candles and the leaf that had landed like a star on his cake, exactly the colour of Miss Gilhoolie's hair. Madeline, happening to glance at him, knew at once that his thoughts were far, far away from Class 4b, Pudding Bag School.

"Miss Gilhoolie," said Samantha. "Look outside. Look at Mr Bedwig with those table-tennis bats. Why is one red and one green?"

"He's waving to something," said Samuel Moon.

"CRIKEY!" shouted Dougal McDougal. "CRIKEY! LOOK!"

"Dougal McDougal!" said Miss Gilhoolie, "Sit down and stop shouting! Everyone, sit down and stop shouting!"

But nobody did. Instead, they rushed to the windows, shouting, and Miss Gilhoolie rushed too, and then she said in a very odd voice, not shouting, "Simon, come here!"

So Simon looked dreamily up from his

diary to see what all the fuss was about.

And out in the playing field an enormous, ancient hot air balloon was just touching down.